Luke checked over his shoulder. Still no sign of the attackers.

This almost felt worse than actually seeing them. If they weren't in sight, Luke didn't know where they were, and he liked to always have an eye on his enemies.

He and Claire crossed not far from where he'd parked when gruff male voices from around the corner made them freeze. Luke yanked her down with him behind the side of a dumpster.

Claire let out a low whimper and shrank into herself. Luke put a hand on her arm and pulled her to his side. But her cat, Kahn, decided he'd had enough of being held and slipped through her crooked elbow. As Claire gasped, Kahn jumped onto a nearby trash can, toppling it with a loud crash.

"What was that?" one of the men asked.

Claire reached out for Kahn, but Luke wrapped his arm around her shoulders and held her back. She loved that cat, but he wasn't letting her get killed for it.

TEXAS BODYGUARD: LUKE

USA TODAY Bestselling Author

JANIE CROUCH

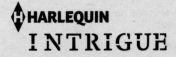

Since this book is about family, it's dedicated to Kiddo #1. What
a talented, beautiful and resourceful woman you've become—you
amaze me constantly. Thanks for making me a mom.

HARLEQUIN®
INTRIGUE™

Recycling programs
for this product may
not exist in your area.

ISBN-13: 978-1-335-58248-5

Texas Bodyguard: Luke

Copyright © 2023 by Janie Crouch

For questions and comments about the quality of this book,
please contact us at CustomerService@Harlequin.com.

Harlequin Enterprises ULC
22 Adelaide St. West, 41st Floor
Toronto, Ontario M5H 4E3, Canada
www.Harlequin.com

Printed in U.S.A.

Janie Crouch has loved to read romance her whole life. This *USA TODAY* bestselling author cut her teeth on Harlequin Romance novels as a preteen, then moved on to a passion for romantic suspense as an adult. Janie lives with her husband and four children overseas. She enjoys traveling, long-distance running, movie watching, knitting and adventure/obstacle racing. You can find out more about her at janiecrouch.com.

Books by Janie Crouch

Harlequin Intrigue

San Antonio Security

Texas Bodyguard: Luke

The Risk Series: A Bree and Tanner Thriller

Calculated Risk
Security Risk
Constant Risk
Risk Everything

Omega Sector: Under Siege

Daddy Defender
Protector's Instinct
Cease Fire

Visit the Author Profile page at Harlequin.com.

CAST OF CHARACTERS

Luke Patterson—One of the four boys adopted as a teenager by Clinton and Sheila Patterson. Before being adopted, he lived at one of the worst San Antonio group homes that was later shut down. Owns San Antonio Security with his brothers.

Claire Wallace—Introverted software designer who spent some time at the same group home as Luke. Likes Khan, her Maine coon cat, much more than she likes people.

Brax Patterson—Most charming and outgoing of the Patterson brothers. Don't let the smile fool you.

Weston Patterson—Most quiet and serious of the Patterson brothers. Often underestimated.

Chance Patterson—Oldest of the Patterson brothers, and the most strategic. The caretaker.

Vance Ballard—Claire's employer and CEO of Passage Digital. Willing to do whatever it takes for power and wealth.

Maci Ford—San Antonio Security's office manager.

Sheila and Clinton Patterson—Adoptive parents of the four Patterson brothers.

Prologue

Everything in this house was clean.

The kitchen had been recently mopped and wiped down to almost sparkling. The bedsheets were freshly laundered; soft, not scratchy like what he was used to. The shower was clean, his clothes were clean, the walls were clean. *Everything* was clean.

But Luke was dirty.

He'd been at the Pattersons' house for a month. Hadn't been hit or kicked by adults or the other three boys who lived here. Kids could sometimes be the most vicious, especially ones feeling like they needed to defend their territory. But not these guys.

Luke had his own room in this giant old house. He definitely hadn't had his own room at the group home. Or on the streets when he'd run away.

And his door locked. Clinton Patterson, the guy here with his wife, had shown Luke how to use the lock.

That was all great, but Luke still put the wooden desk chair under the doorknob every night. It wouldn't keep someone out, but it would at least warn him if someone was trying to get in.

The three other boys living here seemed okay. They were all foster kids, and all close to fourteen like Luke. Luke had seen one of them, Brax—*what a stupid name*—last year for a few days at Skyline Park group home, before Luke had sneaked out again as soon as possible. By the time the cops had caught him and brought him back, Brax was gone.

The other two boys were okay, too. Weston was the quiet Black kid. He hardly ever said anything, but always let Luke play video games with him. The Hispanic kid, Chance, was supersmart. Luke didn't mind him, either.

This place was way better than Skyline Park. It was probably temporary—great foster parents like Clinton and Sheila didn't keep kids like Luke long-term. They adopted babies or sweet blonde angels who floated into group homes for a few months and needed someone to look out for them.

At least that was one good thing Luke had done. Maybe a few months in the Patterson house was his reward for helping out the little girl.

He sat up in his bed and swung his legs over the side. He was hungry. It was late and Clinton and Sheila were old as dirt—like forty or something—and had probably gone to bed. He could sneak some stuff like he'd been doing every night.

Because if being here was a reward, he might as well take advantage of it as long as he could. There were no locks on the pantry or fridge here. There was so much, no one even noticed that Luke was stealing food.

Going to bed *not* hungry had been nice, he wasn't going to lie.

He got up, still fully dressed in sweatpants and a T-shirt, and moved the chair from the doorknob. He padded down the stairs but stopped when he heard Clinton's and Sheila's voices in the kitchen. He was about to turn around and go back to his room when he realized they were talking about him.

He sat on the stairs so he could listen. If they were going to kick him out, it was better if he knew ahead of time.

"I just don't feel like we're reaching him, Clint. Even Weston, with his abuse, didn't take this long for any sort of breakthrough."

"Give him time." Clinton's voice was much deeper. "He's been alone. On the streets and in that group home. We'll get it shut down, don't you worry. Now that social services knows exactly what's going on, they'll make changes."

Sheila gave a shuddery sigh. "I'm just glad he's here where we can keep him safe."

A few seconds later, Luke heard chopping.

"Nothing else bad is going to happen to him. Not while he's in our care." More chopping. "What are you doing?"

"I'm cutting some carrots and celery sticks."

Clinton let out a sigh. "It's after ten thirty at night. Why?"

The chopping resumed. "He comes in every night and gets food. I thought I'd at least make him something nutritious. These vegetables, and I made a sandwich, too. Maybe he'll eat that. I just want him to know he can have all the food he wants."

"I love you, Sheila Patterson." Clinton's chuckle was muffled, like he was saying it with his lips pressed against something. "Luke is going to love you, too. Give him time."

The chopping stopped. "He's been so hurt. He's been on his own too long. He tries to carry too much. He thinks we're going to dump him at the first opportunity. I don't know how—"

"Hey." He cut her off. "Luke is strong. With the right guidance and nurturing, that strength will grow and flourish. He's a protector."

"But he's also just a boy. I want to hug him... I wish he would let me."

Luke couldn't even think of the last time an adult had hugged him. He had no idea what he would do if Sheila tried.

"He will. Someday. When he's ready. Now put that stuff away and let's go to bed."

Luke climbed the rest of the way down the stairs and hid in the dining room until Clinton and Sheila left the kitchen and went up the stairs to their bedroom. Then he slowly walked into the kitchen.

He opened the fridge and grabbed the plate with the sandwich and veggie sticks.

And it was the most delicious food he'd ever eaten.

Chapter One

Claire Wallace wasn't a hero. No one, by any stretch of the imagination, would ever call her one.

Heroes were outgoing and good-looking and quick to take action.

She, on the other hand, was a relatively slow-moving, rather plain, introverted loner who rarely talked to others unless that "person" happened to be her cat, Khan. Khan didn't tend to answer back, but that didn't bother Claire much. She still preferred his company over almost anyone else's.

Right now, she was sitting where she had sat almost every weekday for the past five years since she graduated from college—at her desk at Passage Digital, a software and phone app development company. Most of the people hired five years ago had moved up the corporate ladder at least a little bit. Claire still worked on the third floor with mostly newbs, fresh out of school with their first career-oriented job.

Not being promoted didn't bother her much, either. Getting promoted generally required regularly interacting with other people and getting noticed.

Did she have crippling social anxiety? Yep.

Did she plan to tackle that any time soon? Nope.

A hero she was not. So when her coworker/partial boss, Julia Lindsey, emailed her an hour ago to be at her terminal at 10:00 a.m. and that it would make Claire a hero, Claire had been less than enthused. But here she was.

Maybe she wanted to offer Claire a promotion?

But promotions came with more responsibility, and more responsibility came with increased human interaction, and increased human interaction came with…

Claire pressed a hand to her suddenly tight chest. *Had someone turned up the office's heat?*

Taking a deep breath, she did her best to shake off the bad feelings.

The clock kept ticking. It was only 10:02, but Julia had always been early to meetings; her punctuality was one of the things Claire had appreciated the most while they were working on the camera phone filter app Julia had conceived.

"Hey." Claire reached a hand out toward the guy walking by her cubicle, not quite touching him.

Tom? Trent? Terrance?

Who knew? He'd been working there a couple of years, but the two of them had never spoken.

His eyebrows shot up in surprise. "Uh…yeah?"

Claire cleared her throat, swallowing past the lump. "Have you seen Julia?"

Tom-Trent-Terrance shook his head. "No. Sorry."

Claire nodded and slumped back into her chair.

That had been hard enough. She wasn't asking anybody else.

Julia probably wanted to talk about their cell phone filter app, Gouda. The first version of the app had been hugely popular. The new version they'd been working on—with a much more complex facial recognition matrix—would be able to do so much more.

Teenagers all over the country would be beside themselves with excitement as they were able to morph their faces into all sorts of animals, celebrities and objects.

Or would've, until Julia halted all work on Gouda last week. There'd been no explanation given for the project's sudden stop, which was probably weird.

But, of course, Claire hadn't asked for reasons. She never did.

Today's meeting probably wasn't about the app, anyway. That was over. It was probably related to doughnuts or something. Passing treats out would make anyone an office hero.

Claire's phone beeped with a text from Julia.

Bring a portable drive to my office ASAP. Get on video chat.

Snatching up a portable drive, Claire did as instructed. Julia's office was at the other end of the open work space, nice and private, with windows and its own door—exactly the kind of isolated area Claire dreamed of having.

The office was empty, but the computer screen

wasn't. Julia was already on the video chatting app the two of them had used regularly when working on their filter software. Her dark hair hung limp and tangled while bags underlined her eyes.

Taking a seat at the computer, Claire frowned. Julia was usually so polished.

"Are…are you okay?" Claire hated the way her voice shook.

"Listen, we don't have much time." Julia leaned closer to the screen. It was then that Claire recognized the board table in the background. Julia was in one of Passage Digital's executive offices.

Did that mean she'd been called in for a meeting with CEO Vance Ballard? Was Gouda being green-lighted after all?

Julia licked her lips, seeming to not notice the hair falling in her face. "I don't know who I can trust, but I believe you're out of this entire mess. It's gotten more dangerous than I thought."

Claire's stomach hardened. "What are you talking about?"

"Gouda. Ballard is using it to steal identification and money…from kids. He's creating a database to utilize once these preteens become adults. He'll be able to access their phones and bank accounts."

They'd known this was a possibility with the camera software. Which was why they'd changed it— spent dozens of hours specifically designing it so the pictures that were taken weren't stored.

Claire let out a shaky, disbelieving laugh. "No. We took all those sensitive fields out—"

Julia shot a look over her shoulder at the door be-hind her. "And Ballard put them back in. Hook up the drive. I'm sending you everything that proves Bal-lard has knowledge about what the camera filters do."

Claire's hands shook so much that she wasn't sure if it was physically possible to connect the drive to the USB port.

"I don't think this is a good idea. We don't know what—"

"Claire, we don't have time. Do it. Hurry."

Gulping, Claire did as she was told. Oh yeah, she definitely wasn't hero material.

"We're going to have to go to law enforcement. Ballard doesn't know that I know, so we should be able to—" Julia sucked in a breath and glanced over her shoulder again.

The box with Julia's face went small on Claire's computer. This meant Julia had turned off the picture on her screen—Claire could see Julia, but nobody on the other end could see Claire.

Vance Ballard strode in with two big security guys behind him. "Trespassing in my office, Julia? That's a shame…it truly is."

The Passage Digital CEO's voice was smooth and calm—making it even more frightening. He patted his graying hair as he strolled closer to Julia and the camera. Claire had only spoken to the older man once, muttering an apology when she bumped into him in the hall.

"I just left some papers I needed to pick up. But you're right, I shouldn't have come in here without permission. I'm sorry." Julia sounded nervous and high-pitched—the opposite of Ballard.

"You left papers on my laptop?" Ballard raised an eyebrow. "*Convenient.*"

Claire looked over at the drive. Whatever Julia was sending was still transferring.

It didn't take long for Ballard to realize it, either.

"Oh, Julia, what have you done?" He shook his head and reached for his laptop.

The transfer to the drive stopped. Now Ballard's face took up most of the screen as he typed. At the very edge of what the camera captured, Claire could see Julia backing up until one of the large guards stopped her, holding her arm.

"Looks like you were transferring some pretty important data to your office," he tsked as he turned to glance at Julia.

"I'm not going to let you steal all these people's identities." Julia tried to jerk herself away from the guard, but he held her tight. "And these filters are mostly for children. There are even more laws against that."

Ballard shook his head. "You should've just minded your own business. I gave you the perfect out. Told you I'd take care of it. You should've looked the other way."

He nodded at the man holding Julia and almost before Claire could process what was happening, the man grabbed Julia by the head and snapped her neck.

Claire clapped her hand over her mouth as she

watched Julia's body hit the ground, her eyes still open staring toward the laptop.

"Take care of this." Ballard gestured toward Julia. "Make sure the body is found far away from this building and that it looks like an accident."

Claire pressed a hand to her chest, her heart thumping uncontrollably against her shaking fingers.

Julia was dead.

Ballard had just had her killed.

"Go down to her office and get the drive she was sending the data to. Bring it back up here so I can look through it before destroying it."

Claire had to get out of here. She pressed the key on Julia's computer that downloaded the recorded interactions they'd had on each other's screens.

Including, in this case, Julia's murder.

It went straight onto the Passage Digital hard drive where Claire would be able to access it later.

But something happened on Ballard's end, tipping him off.

"What the hell? That bitch was recording this whole thing?" Claire jumped back as Ballard's face jerked right up to the camera. He couldn't see her, but it sure felt like he could.

"We need to get to her office right away. Damage control."

The monitor went blank.

Claire sat there, eyes wide, trying to draw enough air into her lungs. What should she do?

She could leave the drive, leave the footage of Julia's death on the system, and nobody would know

Claire had been here at all. But as soon as Ballard got hold of the drive and footage, he would wipe them both completely clean—and all proof of his wrong-doing would be gone.

Claire only had two or three minutes tops before Ballard's men got here. If she was going to do something, she had to do it now.

Almost without conscious thought, her fingers were flying over the keyboard. She buried the footage of Julia's murder deep inside the Passage Digital system. When Ballard tried to access it, it would look like a corrupted file—damaged beyond utilization. No link to Claire.

But if she took the hard drive, Ballard would know someone had been here. He wouldn't know it was her, but how long would it take to figure it out? She stared at the drive, about twice the size and weight of a smartphone, still plugged into Julia's computer.

She couldn't let Ballard get away with this. With any of it.

She yanked the cord from the computer and grabbed the drive, then walked to the door. When she opened it, she expected to find the entire third floor staring at her, but no one so much as glanced in her direction.

Keeping her head down, she walked toward her desk. Nobody tried to engage her in any sort of conversation, as usual. Thank goodness.

She wasn't sure what to do. Should she stay at her desk? Wait stuff out? Should she move? Get out of the building?

A voice from her group foster home days floated back into her mind. A voice she trusted. *Luke.* He'd never let her down, always protected her.

If you can walk away rather than fight, then do that. Especially you, kitten.

He'd never walked away from a fight. But for her, his advice had been true then and was true now. She grabbed her purse from her desk drawer, tossed the drive inside it, and walked down the corridor between rows of cubicles.

All she could hear was the thrashing of her own heartbeat in her ears when she saw Ballard's men rush toward her. She couldn't let them take her. She knew what would happen if they did.

But they didn't even so much as glance at her, just brushed right by her, beelining for Julia's office.

Claire didn't look back, just kept a steady pace until she'd made it to the elevator. The doors couldn't open fast enough, and she rushed inside the moment there was sufficient space, pounding the garage-level button with more force than necessary. Once the elevator had begun its descent to the lowest level, she began to shake.

"Come on, come on," she murmured.

Just as Claire stepped out of the elevator, an announcement boomed over the loudspeaker that the building was being locked down due to a possible outside security threat.

She pushed through the elevator doors to the garage before they had a chance to seal her inside, racing toward her car. Once inside, Claire forced herself to drive at a reasonable speed out of the garage and onto the street.

Only after she'd made it onto the interstate did she finally feel like she could afford to breathe.

She'd made it out.

But she knew she was far from safe.

Chapter Two

Luke Patterson rubbed his face and stared at the tall stack of paperwork covering most of his desk. Closing his eyes, he took a long sip of coffee.

Unfortunately, when he cracked his lids, all the papers were still there.

He sighed. "Damn it."

San Antonio Security, the company he'd started with his brothers five years ago here in their hometown of San Antonio, really needed to hire an office manager. The business—everything from bodyguard-type work to situational awareness and weapons training to private investigation—had grown exponentially over the past few years. And rightfully so. Among the four of them, the Pattersons had years of background in both the military and law enforcement.

And they had all learned early on in their lives how the world really worked. How to reads situations and people, how to use people's weaknesses against them when needed.

Having to turn away clients was a good place for a business to be. Buried under paperwork…not so much. But if it meant Luke could work with the three people he trusted most in the world—his brothers—then he'd take it.

He grabbed the top sheet from the most offensively large pile, ignoring the chiming from the bell on the office's front door. Even if he wasn't in paperwork purgatory, no one would expect Luke to meet a client entering the office. Brax liked talking to people, which was why his office was near the front.

Luke was the opposite. He was too gruff, too impatient with people to deal with them on a regular basis. Even Weston, quiet as he was, or Chance, always inside his own head, was better suited to talking with clients than Luke was.

A tap on Luke's open office door a few moments later made him glance up. Brax stood there, a smile playing on the edges of his lips.

"Please tell me that's the fire marshal and we're all being ordered to abandon the building, saving me from this." Luke gestured to his desk.

Brax only smiled wider. Despite the fact that the two of them could be as different as night and day, they were closer than Luke had ever believed possible. Their time together in the army probably had a lot to do with it.

Then again, Luke was equally tight with Weston and Chance, who had skipped the military in favor of careers in law enforcement.

"Someone's here to see you." Brax tilted his head toward the front of the office. "She asked for you by name."

Luke sat straighter. "Who?"

No one ever asked for Luke, especially not women. He couldn't remember the last time he'd been on a date. He blamed it on the business growth, but the truth was he hadn't found a woman he'd felt like he could open up to—one who could even understand his past, much less accept it.

Brax glanced over his shoulder at someone down the short hall. "He said come on in."

"I didn't—"

The rest of the sentence died in Luke's throat as a delicate blonde woman walked into the office, her big blue eyes pinned on him.

He knew her immediately. "Claire."

"Luke." Only one word, but her voice trembled as if she barely had the strength to say his name.

Scratches covered her arms, and she held a big gray cat close to her chest.

The scene was painfully familiar. As a kid, she'd been scratched and bruised way too often, and she'd never gone anywhere without her stuffed cat.

"Looks like you got yourself a real cat." The words were out before Luke gave himself the chance to think them over.

He started to wince, but she smiled. "Yeah."

What now? A handshake? A hug?

Nothing seemed right for the girl who'd never been far from his mind, even though he hadn't seen her in fifteen years.

She loosened her hold on the giant cat, who jumped from her arms and landed gracefully on the chair in front of Luke's desk.

Stepping forward, Claire offered her hand. Her palm trembled against his, her skin cold. Dark circles hung under her eyes, revealing exhaustion and fear.

"What are you doing here?" He forced himself to let go of her hand after briefly shaking it.

Claire withdrew her palm and hugged herself. "I saw you on TV a few months ago."

Behind her, Brax snickered.

"Right." Luke's jaw tightened. "I remember that."

It had been following the successful resolution of a kidnapping case. After a heated custody battle, a preteen girl had been taken by her father, who'd then proceeded to barricade the two of them in an abandoned house. As the Pattersons had been hired by the girl's mom to help locate her, they'd assisted the police in recovery.

A news crew had shown up and stuck the microphone in Luke's face before he'd gotten a chance to duck away. His brothers still made fun of how awkward and stiff he'd been on camera. But it had brought in even more business for San Antonio Security.

"Hey, did we hear the front door chime?" Weston's head popped around the doorway, Chance close behind him.

Claire turned and took a rapid step away from them. The cat jumped into her arms and she clutched it to her, discomfort clear on her face.

Luke cleared his throat. "Claire, these are my brothers, Weston, Chance and—"

"Brax." Brax stepped forward and offered Claire his hand. "I'm the mutt of the bunch."

Most people did a double take when it was revealed the four were brothers. Since Luke was white, Chance was Hispanic, Weston was Black, and Brax was biracial, they looked nothing alike. Brothers, just not by blood.

Claire seemed to take it all in stride. But she wasn't most people. She knew Luke hadn't come from a traditional home.

Brax shook Claire's hand against the cat for an unnecessarily long time. Luke had to swallow a growl in his throat.

Brax never had a problem finding a woman to date. His charm and wit made him pretty irresistible, not to mention his looks.

It was Chance who read the potential disaster of the situation and hooked a hand over Brax's shoulder, pulling him back. "We, uh…have the storage closet to clean out."

Brax's nose wrinkled. "Since when?"

"Since now." Weston tugged on Brax's other arm. "It's nice to meet you, Claire."

Luke could hear his brothers whisper and the whoosh of air as either Chance or Weston no doubt hit Brax in the stomach.

And then he was alone with Claire.

With the others gone, the cat jumped to the floor and sat in front of Claire like he was her guard, his hard gaze locked on Luke.

"That thing looks like a watchdog."

"Khan thinks he's a dog. He's protective." Claire

rubbed him with her foot. The cat looked at Claire, somehow knowing she was talking about him.

"Maine coon, right?"

Those cobalt blue eyes lit up with surprise. "Yeah."

Back when they were kids in their group home, Luke gave Claire the nickname Kitten because she dragged around a stuffed animal cat. Half of what that little girl with braids made of sunshine and eyes cut from the sky talked about was getting a cat one day.

Looked like her biggest dream had finally come true. Despite the exhaustion apparent on her face and the scrapes and bruises, he was glad at least that much had happened for her.

"I'm glad you have someone looking out for you. I always wondered what happened to you." Luke's heart squeezed tight. He'd probably never admit to anyone just how much he'd thought about her.

"After I left the group home, I went into two long-term foster families." Claire shrugged. "It worked out okay."

It didn't have to be added—she never got adopted.

"You?" Her pale eyebrows lifted.

Luke's mouth went dry. He'd only stayed at the group home a handful of days following her departure. She was the only reason he hadn't run away earlier. Claire had a way of always being the kid who got picked on, and she'd needed someone to watch out for her.

"Not long after you left, I was adopted by the Pattersons." He chose to leave the few months on the streets, before he was found and dragged back to the group home, out of the story.

"Oh wow."

"They adopted all four of us. Gave us the chance to take their name if we wanted, and all four of us did." His voice swelled with pride. "Those two gave me a direction. Stability. I owe them my life."

The look in her eyes said it was an experience she couldn't relate to. He pointed to the chair across from his desk and she took a seat. Khan immediately jumped into her lap. Damn thing was nearly half the size she was.

"What about you? What do you do now?" He sat behind his desk, hoping that if he got her talking it would help her to relax. And eventually get her to admit to whatever had brought her through San Antonio Security's doors.

"Software design and programming." She shrugged like it was no big deal, but she was stiff.

"That's great. You always did love computers."

She fell into silence, not saying anything else about her work. But the hand that stroked Khan was unsteady.

He shifted some papers over so he could lean toward her. "Claire, I'm real glad you're here, and you're always welcome to visit… But I get the feeling you're not here to catch up on old times."

She slowly lifted her head, her throat rolling with a swallow. He wanted to leap over the desk and pull her into his arms. Promise her that everything would be okay, that he would help now like he'd tried to help then.

But she looked so fragile, like the slightest touch might break her.

He kept his tone gentle. "You have scratches. A bruise on your cheek."

"I-I was mugged."

"Do you know who did it?" He grabbed a pad of paper so he could write down details, ignoring the fury pooling in his gut at the thought of someone hurting her.

"No, I..." Avoiding his gaze, she licked her lips. "It's been rough lately. I-I kind of started hanging out with the wrong people. I think it has something to do with them. And the guys who mugged me know where I live."

He waited, knowing this wasn't the whole story, but she didn't say anything else. Claire was hiding something, the truth buried in details she wasn't telling.

Not that he needed the full story. Not yet, anyway. She needed assistance, and hell if he wouldn't do anything he could.

"How can I help, Kitten?"

He hadn't meant to call her by that old nickname— didn't even know if she would remember it—but its escape from his lips had been natural.

Claire wrapped her arms around Khan, peering out at Luke from over the protective creature's head. Her voice cracked as she spoke. "I can't go home. The men who mugged me took all my credit cards and some of my cash."

Luke kept his features carefully blank. Muggers stealing credit cards and leaving cash behind was highly unusual. It was yet another sign that Claire hid something, but he wouldn't press for more. Not yet.

Not when she looked like she was going to shatter at any moment.

"When was the last time you got some sleep?"

"I'm not sure." Her voice dropped to a whisper. "A few nights… I didn't know where to go."

Still not the whole truth.

"I'm going to get you a hotel room," Luke said. "I'll pay for it."

She parted her lips like she might protest, but in the end, she nodded. "Okay. Thank you. But I don't want you to think that's why I came here. I'm not trying to use you."

"You're not using me. I'm glad to help out an old friend. Once you get some sleep, we can figure out what to do next."

She smiled, though it wasn't without uncertainty. "Okay. Thank you."

A few minutes later, he had her and Khan bundled into her car and she was following him to a motel a few miles away. He would've liked to put her up somewhere nicer—and closer—but she'd explained that Khan liked to go outside to use the bathroom so it would be more convenient not to stay at a traditional hotel.

Damn cat really did think he was a dog.

He took her to a motor lodge where she could let Khan in and out easily and could park right in front of her room. She waited in her car while he checked her in at the front desk, not wanting the clerk to know she was staying alone.

When he came back out, Claire was staring out her windshield, almost glossy-eyed with exhaustion. He'd planned to take her out to a restaurant to eat and talk some more, but instead, he settled for driving her to a nearby fast-food joint where he made her eat. Greasy calories were better than none at all.

Back at the motor lodge he carried her small bag of belongings as he walked her to the door and placed the bag on the dresser inside. She looked like she was about to fall over. "Get some sleep. Everything will feel better after a night of rest, I promise."

"Thank you," she whispered, sitting down on the bed.

He didn't want to leave her here alone, but sleep was the best thing for her right now. And he'd be much more useful back at the office digging into her situation more thoroughly.

"I'll be back first thing tomorrow morning. We'll talk more then. Lock the door behind me when I leave."

She nodded. "Luke, I—" She stopped whatever she was going to say. "Thank you for helping me."

Unable to stop himself, he softly touched her cheek. "Get some rest, Kitten. You're not in this alone anymore."

Chapter Three

Luke's gaze was stuck to his rearview mirror as he drove away from the motel. Leaving Claire alone went against everything in his gut, but he had to do it.

He needed answers, and at that moment, they weren't coming from her.

At the first stoplight, he put in a call to his friend over at the San Antonio PD, Rick Gavett.

"Gavett." The background sounds of a busy police department undercut Rick's voice.

"Rick, it's Luke Patterson."

"Luke! I usually get a call from Weston, not you. Who do you need found today?"

They'd all known Rick for years, although Weston was closest with him. He'd been on the force with Rick before a bullet during an undercover assignment gone wrong had ended Weston's law enforcement career and almost his life. Rick had always been willing to help out San Antonio Security whenever he could.

"Not trying to find anyone today, believe it or not." Luke looked in the rearview again, even though he couldn't see the motor lodge any longer.

"No one? What, are you guys shutting down San Antonio Security or something?"

"Not while I'm alive and kicking." The light turned green. "I need a different kind of favor from you today."

"Do tell."

"I have an old friend I need to check up on. Name's Claire Wallace." The name tasted achingly sweet on Luke's tongue, like he'd gotten one bite of the best dessert in the world and now wanted more.

"A lady friend?"

"A childhood friend. She's in some kind of trouble and needs my help, but the details are slow coming."

"Claire Wallace. Got it. I'll see what I can dig up later this afternoon when things aren't so crazy. I'll call you soon."

"Thanks. And hey, Rick?"

"Yeah."

"I'd appreciate if you keep this on the down-low." Luke cleared his throat. "Claire isn't the kind to get involved in trouble. Whatever's going on, I don't think it's her fault."

At least, he hoped it wasn't.

He ended the call with Rick and drove the rest of the way back to the office, waiting a second in his truck before getting out.

Everything outside looked normal. No cars with tinted windows cruising by slowly. No one watching from the bus stop bench across the street. But that was because the people waiting to pounce on Luke were already inside.

His brothers were going to have questions, a lot of them. He got out with a sigh and walked to the door.

Sure enough, Luke wasn't inside two seconds before his brothers were all over him.

"Who was that?" Weston, serious as always, frowned in concern. "Why have we never heard you mention Claire Wallace before?"

Chance fired out his question before Weston was even done. "You didn't buy that whole 'stole my cards but not my cash' story. No mugger in the history of the world has ever done that."

Brax held out his hands to calm everyone down. "Guys. Let's start with the most important question… Can I be the flower girl at your and Claire's wedding? Because seriously, I've never seen you be so sweet and soft-spoken with anyone, even Mom."

Chance and Weston chuckled, and Luke rolled his eyes, brushing past them and walking toward his office. "She's a potential client. Can a guy get some space?"

They followed. He knew they would. Ignoring them, Luke sat at his desk and powered on his computer.

"We're concerned." Chance took the seat across from him, the same one Claire had sat in.

"She's an old friend. I knew her when we were at the group home together in Skyline Park before it was shut down."

"Right." Brax leaned against the doorjamb. "The group home. You were there much longer than me, but never talk much about it."

Luke shrugged. He didn't talk about his past because none of it was worth repeating. He'd never known his biological father, and his mother had lost custody of him when he was seven because of the drug problem that eventually led to her death. He'd bounced around foster homes until he ended up at the hellhole Skyline Park at thirteen, and tried to get out of there as often as possible. Living on the streets had been preferable. He'd probably be dead or in prison if the Pattersons hadn't taken him in.

What was there to talk about?

"Why did Claire come here?" Chance asked after it became obvious Luke wasn't going to say anything else. "Have you been in touch with her since the group home?"

"No. I haven't seen her since she was placed with a family when she was eleven. Obviously, she's in some kind of trouble," Luke said. "She won't tell me what. We're supposed to talk more tomorrow."

Chance nodded. "But she specifically sought *you* out after all these years. You must've made some kind of impression on her."

Luke looked up at his most quiet and thoughtful brother and nodded. Had he impacted Claire that deeply? It would certainly be nice to think so. "We sort of looked out for each other at the group home."

"You mean, you looked out for her," Brax inserted. "It looks like a door slamming too loudly could scare that girl."

"Yeah, I guess." Luke nodded thoughtfully, his eyes on the wall. "Claire was younger than me. I was thirteen when she showed up at the home at ten years old. I'd been about to run away again, actually. Had my bag packed and everything."

It had been a plastic shopping bag. The backpack he'd shown up with long gone—stolen by another kid before he'd aged out of the group home.

Luke hadn't had a plan; he just knew staying there wasn't going to work.

A lot of foster homes weren't great, but the group home was terrible. Kids were cruel to each other, stole and fought all the time, and the adults barely paid any attention to what was going on. You had to sleep with one eye open, if you got any sleep at all in the dormitory-style bedrooms.

"But you didn't leave?" Brax went to the window and surveyed the parking lot.

A distant memory tugged on Luke's heart. Little Claire. She'd been so delicate. Ten, but more the size of an eight- or nine-year-old. She'd pulled on every protective instinct Luke hadn't even known he'd had.

"Kids there were the worst of the bunch—most of them unplaceable. Older ones were always looking for someone to pick on, and it didn't take long for Claire to be cast in that role. Her head was always in a book or on a computer. So quiet and shy. A bully's dream."

Only a couple of days after she arrived at the group home, Claire showed up at the breakfast table with bruises and scratches.

Not unlike how she showed up at the office this morning.

A girl always known for starting trouble had been

picking on little Claire—bullying her in ways just short of overt.

Luke wasn't the oldest or biggest kid at Skyline Park, but he knew how to take care of himself and had long since proven no one should mess with him. And for a reason he still couldn't identify, he'd stepped in and helped Claire.

"I helped her out." He shrugged like it wasn't a big deal. But it had been a big deal for them. "She was scared all the time. Boys and girls slept on separate ends of the house, which meant I could only protect her during the day. So I stole some walkie-talkies from the dollar store so we could talk at night."

He looked up from his computer to find all three of his brothers staring at him thoughtfully. He'd never talked about his past this much.

"We checked in every night until she was placed with a family when she was eleven."

Luke's throat constricted. He hadn't realized just how important Claire was to him until she wasn't there anymore. With her gone, the bag came out again. He was living on the streets not even a week later before he was caught and brought back.

Not long after, the Pattersons had found him and offered him a place in their home.

"She meant something to you," Weston said in his quiet way.

Luke scrubbed a hand over his short brown hair. "Yeah, I guess. In a kid way. If she's in trouble now, I'd like to help, too."

Chance stood from his chair. "Then that's what we'll all do."

Luke turned to Weston. "I've already got Rick Gavett running her to see if anything comes up. I'm going to dig into her, too, so I know what we're up against when I see her tomorrow. I'll keep you posted."

He spent the rest of the morning and a big chunk of the afternoon alternating between the paperwork still overwhelming his desk and seeking info about Claire.

The basics were easy to get. Claire had stayed close to home for college, then she started developing software and apps for Passage Digital right out of school. She'd never been married—he refused to even acknowledge whatever feeling it was that zinged through his chest at that info—and had committed no crimes.

Nothing stuck out as particularly notable or questionable.

So, what then? How had Claire accidentally gotten involved in some bad news? Hopefully, Rick would be able to shine more light on that subject because Luke was having no luck, meaning he had no choice but to face the paperwork piles.

The doorbell ringing made Luke look up a couple of hours later, before glancing at his watch. Already nearly five o'clock.

"Can we help you?" he heard Brax ask.

"Are you Luke Patterson?"

"No, I'm his brother, Brax. We're partners in San Antonio Security. Are you looking to hire us?"

"I'm Officer Arellano." He pointed to the shorter

man next to him, who was also in a suit, pulling out a badge and showing it was real. "And this is Officer Fisher. We have a few questions about Claire Wallace."

At the sound of Claire's name, Luke dropped the papers he was filing and zoomed into the waiting area, forcing himself to slow as he walked in. "Afternoon, officers. I'm Luke Patterson."

Arellano's eyes narrowed as Weston and Chance also entered the reception area. "I thought you guys were brothers."

Luke didn't have time for a cultural sensitivity lesson right now. "Did Rick send you over with info?"

Fisher crossed his arms over his chest, ignoring the question. "We're looking for Claire Wallace. Is she here?"

Luke shook his head. "Nobody is here but us right now. Is there a reason you're looking for her?"

"Why don't you let us ask the questions," Arellano bit out.

Luke forced himself to keep a relaxed posture against the doorframe. Something about these guys was off, and he wasn't going to give them any info about Claire until he knew more.

"We know you've been in contact with Claire Wallace today. We need to ask her some important questions."

"She wanted for something?" Brax asked with his friendly smile.

Fisher and Arellano glanced at each other. "We're not at liberty to say. It's in your best interest to let us know where she is."

Like hell it was. If Rick hadn't sent them, then how did they even know Claire had been in contact?

Luke took a step forward. "She was only here for a few minutes."

"What did she want?" Fisher asked. "What did she talk about? You need to tell us everything she said."

Luke shrugged. "She wasn't here very long. Was asking if we had any protection agency contacts for Toledo. It was Toledo, right, guys? Wasn't that where she was going?"

His brothers backed him up with affirmative responses immediately. Luke hadn't had any doubt they would.

"Toledo, *Ohio*?" The tall cop's face folded in annoyance.

Chance perched himself on the edge of the couch. "I know, right? Why would anyone leave Texas to go to Ohio? Sadly, we didn't have any contacts there to offer her."

Arellano's eyes narrowed. "Why'd she come here in the first place?"

Brax hooked a thumb in Luke's direction. "Mc-Dreamy over here was on the news a month ago. Now we're overwhelmed with clients of the female persuasion. Not that we're complaining."

"Sorry we're not more help," Luke said, not at all sorry. He wanted them out of here so he could talk to Rick and find out exactly what the hell was going on. "If you want to leave your card, we can let you know if Ms. Wallace contacts us from Toledo."

The officers glanced at each other again like they

weren't exactly sure what to do with that offer. Just another clue that something was off.

"We'll be in touch if we need you," Fisher said, and they walked out the door without another word.

"What the hell was that all about?" Brax asked.

Luke wasn't sure if his brother meant the fact that there was something completely off about those cops or the fact that they'd just lied to them.

He was saved from answering by his ringing cell phone. Pulling it from his pocket, he saw it was just the man he wanted to talk to.

"Rick. Talk to me."

"Who the hell is Claire Wallace, Patterson?"

The words were so loud, Luke knew all his brothers could hear.

"What did you find?"

"It's crazy. I've haven't seen such red flags in my whole fifteen years of law enforcement. It's like she's a fugitive and there's a statewide manhunt going on for her—all inquiries are sent straight up to the top of the law enforcement food chain to the Criminal Investigations Department in Dallas."

Luke's heart sank. "So she's wanted for something pretty bad."

"You would think so. But that's where it gets really weird. There's not even an official APB on her. She's got no record, and she wasn't even in the Texas Department of Public Safety system until a few days ago."

"I don't understand what you're saying, Rick. Is Claire a wanted criminal or not?"

"I'm saying something really weird is going on, and it's way above my pay grade."

Luke ran a hand through his hair, looking at his brothers. "We just had a visit from a couple of officers. Fisher and Arellano. They legit?"

He could hear Rick type into his computer. "Yeah," he whispered a minute later. "They're Criminal Investigations Division in Dallas. My inquiry must have led them to you. There's something not right about all this, Luke. It doesn't make sense to send someone from Dallas when they could've just sent someone from our office to talk to you."

"Yeah. That doesn't seem right."

"Look, I'll send you what I have on Wallace, although it's not mu—" Rick muttered a curse under his breath.

"What?"

"File on Claire Wallace had been locked. I can't get into it anymore."

Luke had no idea what to say about that.

"Look," Rick finally said. "Someone way high up is looking for this woman and not through normal channels. I'll see if I can find anything else, but it looks like they're closing it down on my end. They'll probably say it's an Internal Affairs issue."

"Thanks for trying, Rick."

"Listen, Luke. This whole thing stinks to high heaven, and now you're right in the middle of it. Until we know what's going on, you guys be careful."

"We will."

Luke hung up and looked around at his brothers,

who all wore matching grim expressions. They'd heard enough to know this had just gotten ugly.

Luke needed answers. They all did.

The quickly falling night drew his attention outside. He wasn't supposed to talk to Claire until tomorrow morning, but this couldn't wait. She was the only one who really knew what was going on.

And it was time for her to start talking.

Chapter Four

"No!"

Claire threw her hand out toward Julia, but it was no use. The other woman slumped against the floor, her eyes open but lifeless.

A force on her waist pulled Claire backward. She screamed and thrashed but it did no good. She couldn't get away from what was dragging her down.

"Mee...rrow."

Claire froze. *Meow*?

In an instant, Julia was gone. Claire opened her eyes. The pressure on her waist was Khan, pawing at her in concern, nothing more. She was in the bed of the motel room Luke had left her in hours ago.

Pressing her palm to her forehead, she found her skin slicked with sweat. Another nightmare. It had happened every time she'd closed her eyes. Sleeping shouldn't be this hard when she was this exhausted.

She'd barely slept since the moment Julia's lifeless eyes had looked out at her from where she'd hit the floor.

Three days since Julia's death, and the terror eating Claire from the inside was only getting worse.

She dragged herself out of bed and into the shower, washing off the last of the nightmare.

The water, as hot as she could stand, washed over her. She was alive, and that was the most important thing.

She had rushed home after fleeing Passage Digital. She knew it wouldn't take them long to figure out she was the one Julia had been communicating with.

She'd parked down the street and sneaked into her house. She needed to run, but there was no way she was leaving without Khan.

She'd thrown what she could in a bag and grabbed any cash she'd had squirreled around the house. She'd been just about to slip out the back door when two of Ballard's men broke in through the front.

"Remember, no guns. When she comes in here, we've got to make it look like an accident."

"Mr. Ballard said the best plan will be to put her with the other body and run a car off a ravine. Won't raise many red flags."

Claire had stuffed her fist up to her lips, so frozen with fear it had taken all her strength to move. *They were really going to kill her.* Somehow, she got herself and Khan back out through the side kitchen door and down the block to her car, although not without bumping into a neighbor's fence and taking a spill that resulted in a bruised face.

From there, she hadn't known what to do other than drive around aimlessly. Nightfall found her outside of Austin, a couple of hours from San Antonio. Wanting to see if Ballard was tracking her, she paid for a room with a credit card, then hid behind the fast-food joint across the street and watched.

Sure enough, it hadn't taken long before the same men who'd broken into her house appeared. They'd gone inside the hotel and Claire had no doubt they knew what room she'd been given—it would be easy for Ballard to hack a computer system.

Claire had gotten back into her car, once again parked down the road, and left. Her little experiment had proven just what she thought it would. Ballard would trace her any time she used a credit or debit card.

She'd slept in her car at a rest area that night—as much as she could sleep, which wasn't much at all.

Not knowing who to trust and being down to her last few dollars, she'd gone to her last foster family's house. The Romeros had cared for Claire through the tail end of high school and still checked in with Claire every once in a while to see how she was doing.

She was running out of money and soon wouldn't be able to feed herself or Khan. Popping into the Romeros' and getting a meal—and maybe a bed that wasn't her car—had seemed like the perfect plan. They'd definitely take her in for a day or two. Give her a chance to rest and figure out a plan.

She'd parked down at the end of the block and had been walking toward their house, rehearsing her story in her head, when she'd realized there was a car at the curb across from the Romeros' house.

They were being watched.

She'd immediately turned to make it look like she

was going to a neighbor's house, then as soon as she was out of sight of the car, had jumped a fence—leading to more scratches and bruises—and run to her car in a panic.

Her entire body had been shaking. Ballard had figured out where she would go before she had. He had resources she hadn't even dreamed about.

He was going to hunt her down wherever she went. There was nowhere she could go where he wouldn't find her. And going to the police without evidence was just going to make it her word against Ballard's.

He was a millionaire businessman with huge ties to the community. He had friends everywhere and was highly influential.

She was…nobody. No friends. No family.

She'd spent another night in her car, in a random apartment complex parking lot, nearly out of gas and hope. When she'd watched the sun come up, trying to keep from having a complete breakdown, a last-ditch plan had come to her.

Luke.

It had been his voice in her mind telling her to get out of Passage Digital.

She'd never forgotten him. Had wondered what had happened to him.

Then she'd seen him on the news a few weeks back, stoic and handsome. The same Luke, but all grown up. Obviously successful and…

No longer Luke Baldwin, like when she'd known him. He was Luke Patterson now.

Of San Antonio Security.

Protection was definitely what she needed, and she prayed maybe he could help her. Protect her like he had when they were kids.

That was, if he even remembered her.

But she hadn't had any other options, so she'd looked up San Antonio Security's office and driven there. She sat in the parking lot across the street for three hours before finally going inside.

He'd remembered her.

He'd helped her.

He'd somehow heated the female parts of her she wasn't even sure worked correctly. Despite her fear and exhaustion, a few minutes in Luke's presence had her more wound up than any of the guys she'd had relationships with during college—all two of them.

She turned off the water and towel-dried her body, getting dressed in one of the two sets of clothes she had left to her name. Then she lay down on the bed, rubbing Khan's gray fur, stretching as she thought of Luke.

No matter how uncharacteristically revved up he'd gotten her, she still hadn't been able to tell him the truth. What if he didn't believe her?

Even if he did buy her story, he couldn't protect her from Ballard. No one could. But he'd bought her a little time.

Khan meowed again and climbed up next to her head on the pillow.

"It's okay, buddy." She scratched the magic spot behind his ears.

A loud purr filled the room.

"You like it here?"

After Luke left, she'd taken Khan outside to do his business and seen the sliding glass door in the adjacent room. With that, Khan would be able to go in and out as he pleased.

All it took was telling the guy at the front desk that her room had a musty smell. He'd traded her key, barely looking away from the TV.

After three days trapped in a car, her precious dog-cat was thrilled to have space and freedom.

"We won't be able to stay long. Sorry. But we'll find a safe place. Somewhere." She didn't know how, but they would.

Claire nestled deeper into the pillows and Khan was finally feeling comfortable. Her eyelids grew heavy, and before she knew it, they couldn't stay open.

Bang!

Gasping, Claire sat straight up in bed. Khan hissed, his fluffy tail swishing against her face.

Had that been a gunshot?

"Police." More banging. "Open the door."

Not a gunshot, the cops knocking on her door. She felt like all the oxygen had been sucked from the planet.

More banging.

But wait… The voice had been too muffled. The police weren't at her motel room; they were at the one next door.

The *first* room she'd checked into.

That wasn't good, either. These "police officers"

hadn't gone to the front desk like real ones would. If they had, they'd have known she switched rooms.

That meant they'd gotten her room info via a computer search—the *Vance Ballard* way.

Unless Luke had turned her in.

No, she couldn't think like that. Not if she wanted to keep it together and not get arrested.

"Ma'am, we're going to need you to open the door."

Claire threw the blankets off her legs. She needed to get out of there.

Grabbing Khan, she slipped on her shoes and grabbed her small purse with the computer drive. The bit of money she still had was in it, along with her car keys.

Not that she could make it to her car, which sat in the front parking lot.

As quietly as possible, Claire opened the sliding door. Thick woods separated the motel and the interstate. She could hide there.

The loud crack of wood made her cringe. They'd broken the door to the room next door. Muffled male voices barked at each other.

It wouldn't be long before they figured out that they had the wrong room.

Holding Khan for dear life, Claire bolted for the woods at an angle away from her predators, in case they looked out the window and spotted her.

She ran as fast as she could, not daring to look back. Cursing at how much time she spent at a computer instead of getting exercise, she was gasping for breath before she even hit the tree line.

Were they behind her? She didn't know. She couldn't hear anything anymore and it was getting dark. The dark would work in her favor.

She had to keep going, just keep putting one foot in front of the other.

Khan was so damn heavy in her arms, but she didn't dare let him down. If he decided to go after some critter, she might not have time to find him again. That was an unacceptable option.

She tucked the squirmy cat up against her and she stepped around a big tree, almost sobbing in relief at the sight of a bridge visible through the woods. If she could get to that, it would take her over the interstate.

She heard sounds behind her. Men talking. They'd figured out she'd come this way. She gulped in a couple of deep breaths, then forced herself to run again.

She'd only gone a few steps before she was stopped mid-stride. Terror engulfed her as an arm wrapped around her waist from behind, lifting her up. A hand pressed hard against her mouth, muffling her scream.

It was just like in her dream earlier, except this nightmare was a reality.

There would be no waking up from this.

Chapter Five

"Kitten, it's me," Luke whispered into Claire's hair, ignoring the sting from that giant cat's scratch. He hadn't wanted to scare her, but he was afraid she'd scream if he just stepped out in front of her.

Her squirming subsided and he loosened his hold so she could turn around.

"Luke?"

"Shh." He put a finger to his lips.

She nodded at his forearm. "Khan scratched you."

"I'll be fine."

"I almost let Khan loose on you." Claire's voice shook.

It sounded like a joke, but the vicious feline could no doubt do some real damage.

"There are men at the motel," she continued. "They said they're the police, but I don't think they are."

"I know." Luke stole a glance around the tree. They were in a good hiding spot for the moment, but they couldn't stay long. Someone had tailed him from the office, and it had taken him a while to lose them without seeming like he was losing them. He'd parked around the corner and walked over. "Cops don't have MAC-10 semiautomatic machine pistols. Those are what bad guys use."

They were close enough that he could feel the shiver come off her.

She had every right to be afraid. Whoever it was breaking into her room had meant business.

"How did you get out of your room?" He took her hand and they walked quickly toward the bridge. He didn't run; right now, stealth was more important than speed.

"I traded rooms so Khan could use a sliding glass door to get in and out."

He picked up speed when they heard shouting not far behind them. They must have figured out what had happened.

"There's something a lot more serious going on than mugging and falling in with the wrong crowd, isn't there?"

She deflated and buried her nose in Khan's fur. "Yes. I'm sorry."

He squeezed her hand. "There'll be time for explanations later. Right now, we need to get out of here. Stay close to me and keep as low as possible."

He moved them forward at a rapid pace, keeping her in front so he was between her and the MAC-10s.

They broke from the trees to the roar of traffic. Cars whizzed by, nothing more than blurs of color. Luke glanced over his shoulder but didn't see anyone.

"When I say run, get to the divide." Luke studied Claire to make sure she'd heard him.

"O-okay."

"Now!" Taking advantage of a break in traffic, they ran for it.

Claire kept up, despite her heavy load with the cat. They made it to the divide, then successfully across the other side of the interstate.

Climbing over the low railing between the road and a Laundromat, Luke checked over his shoulder. Still no sign of the attackers.

Which almost felt worse than seeing them would.

If they weren't in sight, Luke didn't know where they were, and he liked to always have a target on his enemies.

"Where did you park?" Claire adjusted Khan in her arms as they continued.

"Right up here. Half a block." Luke pointed. "Let me carry him for a minute."

She pulled the cat closer. "I don't think he'll let you. He's very protective."

Luke nodded. Now wasn't the time to find out. He quickly moved again, keeping her hand tucked in his.

They crossed behind the Laundromat not far from where he'd parked when a gruff male voice from around the corner made them freeze. Luke yanked Claire down with him behind the side of a dumpster.

"Jennings swears he saw two people cross the highway."

"Jennings also told us she would be in the motel room where she obviously wasn't," another man barked back. "Just because we found her car and stuff in the next room doesn't mean she hadn't run a long time before we got there."

Claire let out a low whimper and shrank into herself. Luke put a hand on her arm and pulled her to his side. Their shoulder blades pressed against the hard brick of the Laundromat. The voices had sounded close, real close.

Khan decided he'd had enough of being held. He struggled in Claire's arms before slipping through her crooked elbow. As Claire gasped, Khan jumped onto a nearby trash can. He didn't quite make the landing, though, and the can toppled over with a loud crash.

"What was that?" one of the men asked.

Claire reached out for Khan, but Luke wrapped his arm around her shoulders and held her back. She loved that cat, but he wasn't letting her get killed for it. He slid them both farther behind the dumpster, peeking through the crack.

Spooked by the trash can, Khan skirted farther into the parking lot, his tail fluffed out in surprise.

A man laughed and hit the chest of the guy who'd pulled at his gun. "It's a damn cat. Come on, there's nobody around here. Let's check out the parking lot and see if anyone is around."

Luke stayed flush against the wall with Claire pressed up against him as the men made their way toward the parking lot. With every breath, Claire heaved against him. She'd buried her face in his chest at some point, and one of her hands fisted his shirt.

Heat rushed through Luke and his heart sped up.

Neither physiological response could be completely blamed on the danger they'd just dodged.

"You okay?" he whispered against her hair.

She nodded, then took a step away from him. "Khan. Come here."

The cat leaped right into her arms, and Luke swore the thing looked sheepish and Claire looked like she was about to lecture the cat about proper behavior.

"Save it," he whispered, taking her hand once again. "You'll have to give the cat a time-out after we're not about to get shot."

Making it safely to his truck a few minutes later only slightly lessened the adrenaline coursing through Luke's veins. He gripped the steering wheel tight as they drove out of the city, his gaze raking the road ahead and behind them for any signs of being followed.

Next to him, Claire looked out the window. Her tangled hair fell in front of her face and her shoulders curved forward like she wanted to disappear.

Luke's chest constricted. He almost didn't want to say anything or ask details about what was going on. She looked so fragile, like the wrong word might break her into a thousand pieces.

But silence wouldn't do, either.

"Were you able to get any sleep this afternoon?" he asked as gently as he could.

"A little."

He turned onto a side road leading out of San Antonio. He wasn't sure where they were headed yet; he just knew that they needed to get the hell out of Dodge.

"Want to tell me what's going on?"

She continued staring out the window for a long minute before she finally spoke.

"I work—well, *worked*, past tense now, I guess— for Passage Digital."

"The software and apps company. Yes, I did a little research on you this afternoon."

She glanced over at him but didn't look surprised. "I developed this business-to-customer mobile application with someone at work. Julia." Her voice cracked on the name.

"Three days ago, Julia told me that our boss, Vance Ballard, had removed certain safety restrictions from our coding. Basically, he made it so that Gouda would illegally collect data from users. That data could eventually be used for financial and identity theft—bank account information, Social Security numbers… pretty much everything."

Luke shook his head. "Hold on. Business-to-customer? And what was that about cheese? The only word I understood was *illegally*."

She gave him the tiniest smile. "Sorry. The program is called Gouda. It's the app Julia and I developed."

"Gouda. Catchy. Okay, keep going. What happened?" He wanted to understand the details more, but that wasn't what was important here. What was important was that she was finally talking.

"Julia transferred Ballard's files to me while we were at work. Evidence we would need to prove what he did. And then…" She lowered her face, nearly burying her nose in Khan's fur. "And then they killed

Julia right in front of me, while we were on video chat. They didn't know I was at the other end or that I was watching. Vance Ballard ordered one of his guys to kill her and the guy just snapped her neck."

He wanted to pull over and stop the truck. Haul Claire into his arms and just hold her.

He muttered a curse under his breath. He had witnessed death in the army, and it had been scarring enough. He couldn't imagine what witnessing the brutal murder of a colleague would do to a person.

He reached over and took Claire's hand where it was balled in Khan's fur. It wasn't enough, but it was all the comfort he could offer for now.

"I was lucky to get out of the building before they realized it was me. I've been on the run ever since. I can't use my credit cards and I'm almost out of cash. Ballard seems to have people watching anywhere I might go to get help or rest."

"Well, he doesn't have anyone watching us now. You're safe, and I'm not leaving you alone again."

Claire nodded, then turned to stare blankly out the windshield. He didn't press her for more info. Her blue eyes had such deep shadows under them that they looked like bruises. The latest adrenaline spike from being chased and almost caught was gone now, and she was bottoming out.

Her physical and emotional reserves were on empty. He'd seen it before in soldiers, and it was never pretty. He needed to get her somewhere immediately so she could rest before she completely broke down.

Going back to the office wasn't an option, and

neither was his house—both were probably being monitored.

Luke pulled out his phone and sent a quick text. He shouldn't have been doing it while driving, but the current situation made stopping the vehicle for even a minute seem riskier.

Couldn't find Claire, she ditched the hotel. I'm taking a few days and going fishing on Calaveras Lake.

"I'm texting my brothers. Telling them I'm off on a fishing trip for a few days." He pocketed his phone. "They'll know it means I'll be off-grid and can't contact them. I hate fishing."

It would also have the people who were undoubtedly monitoring his phone going way out of town to search for him on a huge lake. Luke immediately powered his phone off and took out the battery so there was no way he could be traced.

"Okay," she whispered.

They drove north, in the opposite direction of Calaveras Lake, in the dark. With every rotation of the truck's tires, Luke's mind turned over their predicament.

Where could they go and not be found? Ballard was a powerful man.

Outside of town, he stopped for gas and paid with cash. In case they had to make a quick run for it, having anything less than a full tank would be a dumb move. He grabbed a couple of candy bars while he was in there.

Claire was visibly shaking when he got back in his truck. He peeled open the chocolate bar.

"Here, eat this. Your blood sugar is bottoming out after the chase earlier."

When she didn't so much as move, he gently pressed the candy to her mouth, offering encouraging murmurs as she took tiny bites at a time.

Across the street from the gas station, the lights of a three-story hotel beckoned. Luke wanted to get farther out of town, but Claire was done. She needed to rest.

After paying cash for a room on the bottom floor, he made sure to park the truck where he could see it from the hotel window.

Claire dragged her feet as she walked down the hotel hall. His arms itched to pick her up and carry her, just like she did Khan. Instead, he kept a hand on her arm and slowly led her to their room.

He parked her just inside the door while he checked every inch of the hotel room before he let Claire climb into the bed.

Khan immediately jumped up beside her and curled up against her stomach. When Luke looked back up at Claire's face, she was already asleep, her hand resting in Khan's fur.

Luke scrubbed his face with his palm. The intense day had also left him tired, but sleep wouldn't be easy coming.

Grabbing the armchair from the table, he hauled it over to the space between the bed and the door. If trouble were coming for her, it would have to get through him first.

He ate his candy bar, wincing as she whimpered in her sleep. Bad dreams. If he could wipe them all from her mind, he would, along with everything else that had happened over the last few days.

But he couldn't. All he could do was guard over her, like he had when they were kids. She may be all grown up, but she was still fragile, still needed a protector.

He couldn't stand to think about what might have happened to her if she hadn't escaped Passage Digital. And then all those risky moments between then and now...

His hands fisted. Claire was with him now, and no one was going to hurt her.

Not on his watch.

Chapter Six

Ballard leaned back in his chair, closing his eyes for a moment. When was the last time he'd enjoyed a solid, uninterrupted night's sleep?

It was definitely before certain treacherous employees, who didn't know the value of keeping their mouths shut, decided to poke around in matters that did not concern them.

When his eyes opened, his gaze immediately fell on the spot on the floor where Julia's body had fallen. No blood. Brooks was good that way—a professional, efficient, somebody who did what needed doing without asking questions or allowing personal feelings to muddy the waters.

If only all his associates shared that professionalism.

He should've known Julia wasn't the only weak link. And she was clever, too. He had to give her credit for that. A shame to lose such a brilliant mind, all because her brilliance hadn't lent itself to self-preservation.

In the end, she hadn't even come up with a solid

reason for lurking in his office. Julia had not been a practiced liar since her excuse had been almost juvenile.

It was Claire who interested him these days. Having evaded him, Claire seemed to be somewhat better at lying, at least for now. She couldn't run forever, not with so many eyes on her every move.

The knock at his office door didn't come as a surprise. "Enter." He sat up and straightened his tie while the door swung open and the pair he'd expected joined him. They stood before him, knowing better than to take a seat unless offered one.

He looked from one to the other, noting—not for the first time—how similar the men were in build and mannerisms, right down to their crew-cut hair. Both were men of few words, too, which suited Ballard. "Talk to me."

Brooks and Masters exchanged a look that didn't go far toward granting confidence. "There's not that much to tell, sir," Brooks said in his deep growl.

"Not that much to tell?" He blinked, looking from one to the other. Waiting for one of them to crack. People always cracked when pressed hard enough in just the right place. "How can that be?"

"She got away." Masters remained with his hands clasped behind his back, but beads of sweat at his temple told a story of nerves…of cracking under them.

His blood pressure began to rise. He knew it from the telltale roaring in his ears. "How?"

"We don't know." Brooks lifted his thick shoulders.

"I'm sorry, sir, but those are the facts. When the men entered the room, she was gone. She left her things behind, too."

"The drive?"

"No, I'm sorry. They turned the place upside down." As if that made it better.

Control. He took several deep breaths. His men waited, silent, probably wondering if and when he would explode in rage. How was the girl a step ahead of them? She was nothing! One single girl who all but faded into the background. He hadn't recognized her face upon examining her ID badge and the photos compiled by his team after her escape. She might as well be no one, a nonentity.

Yet she'd managed to escape. Again.

"Why did she go to San Antonio Security?"

"I spoke to Arellano after the visit to their office but he didn't have anything concrete about that." Brooks exchanged another shrug with Masters. "They're either good liars or they were telling the truth."

"The truth being…?"

"That they didn't know her."

"It was probably a last-ditch effort on her part," Masters added, eager to sound insightful and useful after delivering bad news. Ballard was not a man who took bad news easily. "One of the guys from the agency was on TV recently and it upped their visibility. Otherwise, they were all firm on not knowing her or anything about why she came in."

"There's no connection between her and the firm's partners?"

"None that Arellano could find, and you know how thorough he is."

Motivation would do that to a man. Find the right pressure point, and the impossible suddenly became commonplace. Ballard doubted the detective would leave a single stone unturned.

Though that certainty did little to help at the moment. There was still the problem of the girl, where she'd gone and whether she was receiving help. She had to be.

If ever there'd been a poster child for solitude, it was that girl. A lifelong loner. For her to reach out to anyone meant she was desperate. She knew the stakes. Her awareness, her watchfulness spoke of understanding as well.

There had to be an end to her resourcefulness.

Brooks cleared his throat. "What direction do you want Arellano and Fisher to take?"

"I want eyes on their office, these Pattersons. Ears on their phones, as well. Whether there's any connection or not, now that she knows we're able to find her, she'll look for any port in a storm." Masters nodded and left the office, presumably to pass the word to the detectives overseeing the police aspect of this unfortunate dustup.

"What next?" Brooks asked, standing at the ready. Ballard knew through experience that his right-hand associate was up for anything. No request was too large, nothing too far outside the realm of what he was willing to do—like for instance, the Julia problem.

Ballard tented his fingers beneath his chin, staring at the wall over the man's shoulder, seeing the entire situation laid out before him. Like a chessboard, the pieces were already in play. He saw the various parts of Claire's small, uneventful life. The people from her past whom his men were already watching in case she ran to them.

It wasn't enough to wait for her to make a move.

She had to be forced into one.

Yes, it was all so clear. Put his pieces in place, wait for her to make one move after another. No matter what she decided, he would be ready.

A smile spread slowly as everything fell into place. "It's time to turn up the heat under our target," he decided. "Make it so she has nowhere to turn without being noticed. Remove whatever sense of security she still possesses."

"And how do we do that?"

His smile widened. "Oh, that won't be difficult."

IT ONLY TOOK a second for Claire to remember where she was when she woke up the next morning. It took longer when a glance at the clock told her she'd been asleep for nearly thirteen hours.

Even before Julia's murder, she hadn't slept this soundly. One look at the man sleeping upright in the chair next to the bed told her why. Her subconscious had trusted Luke to protect her.

The way he'd always protected her.

She sat up, the bed frame groaning as she moved. In an instant, Luke was awake, his brown eyes trained on her.

"Sorry," Claire whispered. "I didn't mean to wake you."

It couldn't have been comfortable sleeping in that chair, but he stood with no stiffness and with two steps, was at the side of her bed. Claire's breath hitched in her throat. His eyes were serious, face drawn tight, but when he touched the back of her hand, the gentleness there made her head spin.

"Feeling better?" Luke drew his fingers back way too soon.

"Yes." Her voice sounded funny. Did she always talk like she couldn't pronounce words right?

"I'll take Khan out and look for any problems. How about you take a shower?"

"Okay. Thank you."

The hot water had her feeling somewhat human again. She didn't linger, unsure of how long Luke would be gone.

She made a face as she put back on yesterday's clothes. She'd gotten out with the computer drive and Khan.

And her life. She'd just have to be thankful enough for that.

She came out of the bathroom and found Luke standing at the window, peeking at the parking lot through the curtains.

Khan meowed at the sight of Claire, except he didn't come to her. He rubbed against Luke's legs.

"Wow." Claire stared. "I've never seen him do that to anyone but me."

"I got him some beef jerky from the gas station."

Luke's smile made her stomach do a flip, despite her traitorous cat.

Claire kept on rubbing her hair with the towel, even though it had never been thick enough to take long to dry. Her hands just needed something to do.

"What now?" she asked.

The smile disappeared, his lips drawing into a thin line. "We keep moving. First, we'll need to make a stop to buy some stuff."

"Yeah, I'm going to need another change of clothes, if possible."

"Me, too. And some other stuff. We can stop at a superstore. I have some cash."

She grimaced. "I'm going to keep a list of what I owe you."

"That's really not necessary."

"It is to me."

He was already doing so much for her that she'd never be able to pay him for. Case in point, sleeping in a chair and watching over her so she could get the rest she needed. What was the price tag on that?

She would damn well pay back what she could. The idea that he possibly thought she was using him crushed her.

"Okay." He nodded, his brown eyes still somber. "If it's important to you, you can keep track and pay me back."

"Thank you."

He respected her feelings. That meant more to her than he could know.

He led her back out to his truck, opening the door for her. Khan jumped in and she climbed in behind him.

"Where are we going to go?"

Luke started the truck and pulled out of the parking lot. "I spent a lot of time thinking last night."

While he was guarding her. "Thank you for letting me rest."

He glanced at her briefly before turning his eyes back to the road. "You needed it."

Her hopes sank. That wasn't anywhere close to a romantic declaration, not that she'd been expecting one. But she needed to face the facts that maybe this attraction was completely one-sided.

"What were you thinking about last night?"

"Your best bet now is to go to the police."

She flinched and turned toward the window. Would the cops even believe her?

She was about to argue her point when her stomach growled loudly, the sound filling the cab.

"Hungry?" He looked over at her again, one eyebrow raised. "Let's get something to eat and we can talk about this more."

A few minutes later, he slowed the truck and turned into the parking lot of an old-timey diner.

The place, full of shiny countertops and red vinyl booths, felt warm and inviting. Khan had to stay out in the truck, but the weather was mild, so they left the windows cracked and the cat sleeping on the floor.

"Over there." Luke headed for the booth in the far corner, by the kitchen.

He waited until Claire slid in, then took the booth facing the door.

"Going to the police makes sense…" He trailed off as a waitress approached.

"What can I get you two today?" The older woman smiled at them both.

Luke didn't even look at the menu. "Whatever your most popular dish is. And coffee."

"Same," Claire said. "Please."

"All righty." The waitress collected the menus. "Eating the same dish. What a cute couple."

Claire could feel the heat crawl up her cheeks, but Luke didn't even seem to notice the comment. The second the waitress was gone, he rested his arms on the table and leaned into them.

"The police can help. You witnessed a murder." He kept his voice low. "That means there's a body somewhere."

Claire choked on her breath. "But what if they don't believe me? I don't have the footage of Julia's death with me; I had to hide it on Passage Digital's servers. It's possible Ballard found it and deleted it."

She dropped her gaze to the table. Talking about this was so hard.

He reached over and grabbed her hand. "I'll be honest, that could be true, and if it is, Ballard might not be convicted. But if you go to the police, show them what you have about the Gouda app and tell them Julia was killed…it throws a lot of suspicion in Ballard's direction."

"But what if they don't believe me?"

They were interrupted by the waitress bringing their coffee, and Claire was glad to have the distraction. She wasn't sure if going to the police was the best plan or not.

Luke took a sip of his steaming brew. "Why didn't you go to the cops as soon as you got out of the building once Julia was killed?"

She stirred creamer into her coffee, then brought it up to her lips. "My head wasn't on straight. All I could think about was getting to Khan and getting him out before they got to him. Plus, the police were always the enemy when we were kids."

His eyes narrowed behind his cup. "You had run-ins with the police?"

"No, not me."

Awareness dawned. He leaned back in the seat. "I had run-ins and filled your little head with stories about the big bad officers of the law."

She shrugged. "I guess it tainted my opinion. I've never trusted cops."

"You know that was just me talking fourteen-year-old smack, right?" He shook his head. "Not a single police officer who picked me up when I ran away ever did anything to harm me. Most of them got me some food and tried to talk to my sullen ass, not that it helped. Two of my brothers went into law enforcement for a while. I have the highest respect for them and the people they worked with."

She sighed. "I should've gone to them first thing. It's too late now."

They were stopped again by the delivery of their breakfast platter, though Claire had lost her appetite.

He bit into his scrambled eggs, then pointed to her

plate with a piece of toast in the other hand. "Don't even think about not eating that."

He was right. She had to eat. She took a bite of her eggs, then continued to eat as he watched her like a hawk while wolfing down his own food.

He was completely finished before she'd even made it halfway through her meal—except for the piece of bacon he'd put in his napkin. She knew it was for Khan and tried to ignore the things it did to her heart that he was thinking about the well-being of her cat.

"The most important thing is to keep you alive. The people after you—they have instructions to make sure you're not alive to talk to anyone."

She handed him a piece of bacon to add to the collection for Khan.

"Going to the cops and raising as much ruckus about this as possible will make it harder for Ballard's men to take you out without causing suspicion," he continued. "Ballard is powerful, but he's not God."

She lifted her fork to her mouth but then set it back down without eating. There was no way she could keep it down. She wanted so badly to believe what Luke was saying.

"I'll stay with you through it all. I'm here to help you." He reached over and grabbed her hand, running his fingers across her knuckles.

Tears filled Claire's eyes. "Thank you. I'll do it. But are you sure? This is so dangerous."

"It's nothing I'm not used to," he said with zero hesitation.

Claire's laugh was ragged. She seriously doubted his workday involved running from men with assault weapons.

"You came to me for help. This is my job. And besides, it's you."

She didn't have the nerve to ask what that last part meant.

She looked at what was left on her plate. "I wonder if Khan would eat the eggs. He's not very picky. We could get a to-go box."

Luke smiled. "Khan's a very lucky cat-dog."

"He's my family. My only friend." She cringed at her pathetic words, immediately wishing she could take them back.

"That's not true." Luke's brown eyes softened, but they turned to steel a second later. His thick brows knit together, his attention on something behind her.

Turning in the booth, Claire found the TV screen mounted on the diner's wall. It was on mute, captions scrolling the bottom of the screen while a reporter talked.

She gasped when she saw the picture in the upper corner of the screen.

It was *her*.

The shot was from a Passage Digital picnic a few months earlier. She wouldn't have gone at all if it hadn't been basically required.

Wanted for the murder of coworker...

She couldn't stop reading the caption running under her photo.

Authorities are asking for anyone with information on Claire Wallace to contact them immediately...

Claire's mouth filled with chalk, the food she'd eaten threatening to come back up.

"Come on," Luke gritted out in a low voice. "We need to get out of here."

Nobody in the diner was paying much attention to the TV or them, but all it would take was a second and they might.

"I-I…" Oh no. She was going to lose it right there in this booth.

"Look at me, Kitten."

His words, his brown eyes, brought her back. Grounded her. "We're going to make it through this. Keep your head down and stay close to me."

They stood and he wrapped an arm around her, pulling her close. He handed her the bacon in the napkin.

Each step to the exit was a nightmare. Several people glanced at the TV between bites. Had they noticed her? Had anyone called the police?

She leaned into his chest, breathing in his scent.

"That's right. Just act like there's nowhere else you'd rather be than cuddled close to me."

No acting necessary.

She felt his lips against her hair. "We're going to make it through this," he repeated before paying and ushering her out the door.

She felt frozen, even though the fall air was mild.

Making it through this seemed impossible now.

Chapter Seven

Luke didn't waste time getting them out of the parking lot once they were in the truck, but it was all a blur for Claire.

Khan immediately jumped into her lap to get the bacon he could smell through the napkin. She unwrapped it and began to break it into pieces, barely aware of what she was doing.

She watched while he gobbled it up. Hot tears stung her eyes. The days where she and Khan could count on regular meals and the safety of their home were long gone. It could be that they'd never return to their little cottage with the cozy window seat and sunny back porch.

She was well and truly a fugitive now.

"What am I going to do?" she whispered.

Luke's knuckles were white against the steering wheel. "It was a smart play on Ballard's part. Make it so you can't go to the police. It puts you on the defensive, not to mention legitimizes the reason he's had police looking for you."

None of that made her feel any better.

Luke drove, keeping to side roads, his gaze constantly sliding to the rear and side mirrors to check for people following them. He reached into his jacket pocket and pulled out an older-model cell phone.

"Here. I need you to dial a number for me."

"Whose phone is this?"

"I borrowed it from someone in the diner… When I saw one that didn't require a pass code, I couldn't resist. We can't take a chance on using either of our phones. It could lead Ballard right to us. I'll make sure it gets returned."

She shrugged. "You're probably doing the person a favor so he or she can upgrade."

She dialed the number he gave her and then pressed the speaker button, handing it back to him. Luke laid the phone on his leg as it rang.

"Gavett." The voice on the other end was hurried and gruff.

"Officer Gavett. We spoke earlier about a locked computer file? I was wondering if we could talk again." She noticed Luke was careful not to use either of their names.

There was silence on the other end for a few long moments. She started to worry the officer didn't know who it was or maybe didn't care now that she was a fugitive.

"Yes," Gavett finally said. "I need a few minutes. I'll call you back on this number."

He hung up and she looked over at Luke. "Was that a bad sign?"

"Do you mean is he going to try to trace our location? I don't think so. My brother Weston saved his life when he was on the force."

The cell phone rang a few minutes later. Luke once again put it on speaker. "Rick?"

"Patterson. I had to leave the office to make this call. Had to find an honest-to-God pay phone, and let me tell you, not many exist anymore."

Luke's jaw flexed. "That doesn't sound like good news. I'm not trying to get you in trouble."

"After what Weston did for me, whatever you need is worth it. You in a private space?"

Luke glanced over at her. "Claire is here. We're on the road."

Rick was silent for a moment. "You sure we shouldn't talk alone for a few minutes?"

Claire caught his eye. "It's okay," she whispered.

How could she possibly blame Luke if he felt like he needed to talk to his police officer friend without her listening in?

Luke shook his head. "She didn't do it, Rick. She didn't kill Julia Lindsey. Her boss, Vance Ballard, did. Claire is a witness."

Rick let out a loud sigh. "Well, the mandate to find her is coming all the way from the top of the Texas law enforcement chain. Through the same office of the guys who paid you a visit yesterday—Arellano and Fisher."

Claire caught her bottom lip between her teeth. Cops had questioned Luke yesterday?

"What's that mean?" Luke asked. "Are they dirty?"

"I don't think so. But this whole thing feels wrong. It's got a political flavor to it, like someone is using Texas law enforcement for their own personal vendetta—especially if you're assuring me Ms. Wallace didn't have anything to do with the murder."

Claire stopped chewing her lip long enough to speak up. "Vance Ballard is powerful. He would probably have friends very high up the chain. They may not be corrupt, but they would be more willing to listen to what he says about me because they know him."

"Right," Rick agreed. "The problem is, I'm the only one who was looking into you before all this went down. I'm the only one who knew your file had been locked and that there was something not right about this entire situation."

"How bad is the evidence?" Luke asked.

"Bad. And there's nothing I can do for you from my level. Even if I started to shout that something smells fishy, I don't have any proof of any wrongdoing. Bottom line is, watch your back because there's a giant target on it."

Claire caught Luke's eye. He offered what was probably an attempt at a reassuring smile, except it looked more like a grimace.

"Roger that, Rick."

"I've got to go." There was the sound of muffled voices on Rick's end. "I'll email you the files I have on the evidence in about ten minutes. But it won't make you happy."

Luke nodded even though Rick couldn't see him. "Thanks for everything. Take care of yourself."

Hanging up, Luke passed the phone to Claire. Mute, she took it.

Fifteen minutes later, they stopped at a higher-end hotel—one that had a business center where he could access his email and print the files Rick had sent.

Claire knew by the look on his face as he came back out that it wasn't good. Like Rick had said, he wasn't happy.

He handed the printouts to her as he pulled back onto the street.

Reading the printouts soon had everything she'd eaten at the diner curdling in her belly. Ballard had created a fake email chain that made it look like Claire was jealous of Julia because of her position at Passage.

Her tongue had become impossibly heavy. "It's all false."

Tears blurred her vision. It was a good fabrication. It looked like Julia and Claire had messaged back and forth multiple times, with Claire accusing Julia of stealing her ideas. Claire came across as bitter and ugly—warning Julia to "watch her back," and that she would make sure the emails would never be found by anyone.

Then Ballard had swooped in like the hero and dug them up.

The papers shook in her hand as she read it all again. "It makes me look unstable. But the chain is reasonable with just enough detail without going overboard. He probably took real emails between me and Julia and just changed the content."

Ballard had manipulated it to make it look like the communication started weeks ago and then escalated.

"That can be done?"

"Not by most people." She closed her eyes, wishing it would all go away. "But by Ballard, yes."

He had to be applauded. He'd done a fantastic job making it seem Claire had reason to kill Julia. If Claire read this, she'd believe it, too.

Luke continued to drive them farther out of town. "It gives proof of motive. That's all Ballard needed right now."

"There's no going to the cops now." Hot tears pressed against her closed eyelids. "No one will believe me. I don't even understand why you do… You don't really know me."

Luke's silence just added to her fear.

Maybe he thought she'd lied to him. Could she really blame him?

Abruptly, the truck slowed down.

Claire opened her eyes to find they were entering a wooded area. The sign read Government Canyon State Natural Area.

She tensed, papers crumpling in her hands. Was he planning to leave her here?

Again, she couldn't really blame him. Like Rick had said, she had a target on her back and staying with her would put one on Luke's back, too. Not to mention anything he did to help her was illegal.

She couldn't bring herself to ask what he was going to do.

By the time he pulled into the nearly empty parking lot and turned to her, she wasn't sure she was going to be able to keep it together.

"Luke, I—" She wasn't sure what she was going to say, just knew she needed to say something.

"Let's go for a walk—let Khan get some fresh air and exercise."

They walked along one of the many paths, stopping when they got to a picnic table.

"Luke," she started again. "I know it looks bad. I know you must wonder if I'm lying to you, and rightfully so."

He turned and climbed up onto the picnic table, sitting on the table itself. "Do you know what I remember most about you from Skyline Park?"

She shook her head.

"Well, I mean, besides those big blue eyes that were always studying everyone from afar. You never liked to talk to anyone. And you always tried to get on the computer—not that the bigger kids gave you much of a chance."

She shrugged. "I was too young to do much computer-wise then anyway. That's what you remember? Me on the computer?"

"No, what I remember is you sneaking your snack money into Amelia Whalen's backpack."

Claire felt her face burn. "She needed it. She stayed after school and always got hungry. Her stomach used to growl at night. I was never hungry, so I didn't need the money."

The side of his mouth pulled up in a smile. "Even though you never liked talking to anyone, you were always aware of what was going on around you, even as a little kid. And you did something about it."

She swallowed hard, her throat burning. "Anyone would've done it."

He reached out and snagged her hand, pulling her over until she was standing between his knees where his feet rested on the picnic bench.

"No." His voice was firm. "They wouldn't. I've been around a lot of people, both when I was a kid bouncing from place to place before the Pattersons, and in the army. I've learned how to read them. How to judge intentions and purposes. Little Claire had no reason to help Amelia Whalen, especially not secretly."

"I'm not little Claire anymore."

She stared down at where Khan had come to rub against her legs, sensing her distress. She shifted her gaze back up to his when his finger tilted her head gently under her chin.

"No, you're definitely not little Claire anymore... but your heart is still the same. Still generous. I've learned to trust my instincts, and they're telling me you're one of the good guys."

She parted her lips, unsure of how to respond. Luke

had helped her so much already. Him putting his faith in her now wasn't something she took lightly.

"Thank you," she whispered. "I want to prove it wasn't me who killed Julia."

He leaned his forehead against hers. "We will."

His lips touched hers, softly, briefly, before pulling away. All she could do was stare at him.

He actually growled at her. "Staring at me with those big, beautiful eyes is just going to get you kissed again, Kitten."

Was that supposed to scare her off? She tilted her head and raised an eyebrow at him.

He chuckled. "So, the kitten has little claws."

He slipped his arm around her waist and yanked her closer. She laughed breathlessly as her body fell against his.

Then he kissed her for real.

His lips were gentle but firm, commanding but careful. So perfectly Luke.

Claire scooted up onto her knees on the bench between his legs, wrapping her arms around his neck as one of his hands gripped her waist firmly and the other trailed along her spine.

She'd dreamed about this kiss for years. Even when she hadn't been old enough to really know what kisses were supposed to be, she'd known that she'd wanted her kisses to be with Luke.

This one didn't disappoint.

He kissed her with shattering absorption, as if he couldn't get enough of her. His tongue invited hers to play, to dance. His teeth nipped at her full bottom lip gently before soothing the sweet hurt with a gentle lick.

They were both breathing heavily by the time they broke apart. This wasn't the time or place to get lost in each other.

But now she had even more reason to clear her name.

More kisses with Luke.

Chapter Eight

The feel of Claire's lips and that sexy little breathless moan she made as he kissed her were still in the forefront of Luke's mind two hours later as he paid for his purchases at a local superstore.

The cashier popped her gum as she scanned his items. Some food for both them and Khan, a change of clothes for the both of them, a brunette wig for Claire, and a prepaid cell phone he could use without worrying about tracing.

Burner phone.

Luke scrubbed a hand over his face. He definitely hadn't been expecting to need burner phones when this week had started.

If the cashier found his collection unusual in any way, her popping gum never let on to the fact. She looked more bored than anything as she placed each item into the bag after scanning it.

Good. Bored meant she wasn't paying attention and made him much more forgettable.

She told him his amount. "Card or cash?"

"Cash." Luke pulled out his wallet and handed her some bills.

This stuff wasn't cheap. He had enough to cover it, but between paying for last night's second hotel, gas and all this with cash, he was now officially running low.

Turning away from the cashier as she counted the money and put it in the drawer, he looked out the store's window. His truck sat close to the front where he could access it easily, Claire's blonde head tucked low in the window.

He hadn't wanted to leave her out there with just Khan as protection, but that was a better option than taking a chance on her being recognized in the store. Plus, she was already coming up with some ideas on how to fight back against Ballard.

A smile tugged at Luke's lips. That big brain of hers. He had no doubt she would figure out how to access the data she needed to prove her innocence.

And he was going to provide her with whatever help she needed.

Taking the bags, he hurried out of the store. Claire sat up straighter when she caught him approaching and gave him a little wave. He smiled but couldn't stop staring at her lips.

He wanted another kiss. Forget the fact that his arms were full of items that were supposed to help hide them from a law enforcement hunt.

Focus, Patterson.

His focus was something he was usually known for. But something about Claire Wallace blew his focus to hell.

He opened the door and tossed the bags in beside him.

"Are you okay? Any problems?"

He reached over and squeezed her hand before starting the engine. "You're the one who has her picture all over the news, and you're worried about *me*?"

She shrugged. "I can't stand the thought of anything happening to you."

He leaned over and stole a kiss. Just a brief one, afraid that if he let his lips linger, they might start a show right here in the parking lot that would get them arrested for nothing having to do with her fugitive status. He kissed her forehead before he moved back into place and started the truck.

"Did you get everything we need?" Claire asked, putting the plastic bags on the floor near her feet.

He drove out of the parking lot, careful not to draw any attention to them. "Yes. I think you'll look good as a brunette."

She made a face. "I guess so. Did you get cat food?"

"Are you kidding? I'm not taking any chances on that cat-dog chasing me down a back alley because I forgot."

"Good. He can't keep living on bacon and beef jerky."

She looked through the bag. "You didn't use a credit card, right? I should've mentioned that before. Ballard is definitely watching for movement on mine. He's probably watching yours, too."

"No, I used cash. I always carry a pretty good amount with me—a by-product of growing up so long without any money at all."

For years he'd tried not to carry so much, refusing to let the past dictate his present. It was his dad who'd finally sat him down and told him that not everything about his past needed to be fought. If carrying cash helped his subconscious be at ease, then carry the damn money.

Fight the real wars, not the cosmetic ones.

She tried on the brown wig. "How do I look?"

He glanced over. "Good. I like your natural look better, but this helps you blend in a little more."

He didn't even say anything when his truck smelled like cat food a few minutes later when she cracked open a can for Khan.

But they were going to have to come up with a plan. Driving around increased their chances of being pulled over.

"I think I know what I need to do," she said after Khan finished eating. "I have the drive with the info that proves Ballard planned to use Gouda for illegal purposes…" She looked out the window, her fingers twisting in Khan's fur as he settled on her lap. Luke knew that meant she was thinking, so he gave her time.

"Thing is," she started up again suddenly, "the data can't be read outside of Passage Digital because of the proprietary coding we use."

"Can you find a way around that?"

She nodded. "I think I can build a shell program robust enough to extract the information. It won't be perfect, but it will be proof enough to get the police looking into Ballard and Passage Digital."

"Okay. That's good news. What do you need?"

Luke bypassed the turn onto the highway in case they needed to stay in town. "Special equipment?"

"No, it's all coding based. I need a computer that's on public Wi-Fi, so I can make it more difficult to find where I'm located, with uninterrupted time and nobody else around."

"How much time?"

She grimaced. "It's hard to say exactly, but it won't be short. A few hours."

"We'll be too noticeable at a coffeehouse or hotel lobby for that long. We'll have to break in somewhere."

"That might bring the cops straight to us."

It wasn't a perfect plan. Hell, it wasn't even a *good* plan. He would much rather have a few days to scope somewhere out to see if they had alarms or security. Or go somewhere he was familiar with and could protect her more easily.

A location came to mind. One where he'd watched out for her when they were kids.

"How about the Wars Hill library?" He watched for her reaction.

A little smile lit her face. "That would be perfect."

Of the limited time they'd had together when they were young, a lot of it had been spent there. She'd stayed at the library until closing just about every evening. Book time. Computer time. Avoid the group home time.

Once Luke had discovered where she was disappearing to, he'd begun joining her. At first, he was only looking out for her.

But Claire, who'd read way above her grade level,

started recommending books to him. That library, waiting for her to finish on the computer so he could walk her home each day, was where he'd developed a love for reading.

The next time Brax wanted to tease him about staying in with a book on a Friday night instead of going out and having fun, Luke would tell him to blame Claire.

At the next red light, he turned south in the direction of the library. He drove by it often enough to know the building hadn't changed much. But more importantly, he was familiar with it and would be better able to keep watch there.

"It's a plan," he said. "We'll park a pretty good distance away, get there before it closes, and hide. That's better than trying to break in."

He glanced over at her and she smiled at him, her brown hair not right, but still beautiful. "Maybe by this time tomorrow, this can all be over."

Chapter Nine

The library hadn't changed much in the past fifteen years. The puffy blue couches in the children's section had been reupholstered but were the same. The glass study rooms in the back hadn't changed much, either.

They'd parked the truck a quarter mile away—he hadn't wanted to take any chances on it being spotted near the library. Claire hadn't wanted to leave Khan behind. A backpack Luke had forgotten about and found stuffed under one of the truck's seats did the trick. Nestled in there, with the top unzipped a bit for air, the cat only meowed occasionally.

It was impressive, really, the amount of trust that animal had in his human. Then again, she'd no doubt worshipped the little furball from the start.

Kitten.

Luke smiled to himself. Claire was definitely more of a kitten than Khan was.

They slipped in separately about an hour before closing, long enough ahead of time so the librarian wouldn't be paying attention. Claire headed back to the fiction section and Luke ended up in poetry.

He was the least poetry-reading guy he'd ever known but forced himself to crack open a book anyway. Walt Whitman wasn't so bad.

A mom with three young kids came in about twenty minutes before closing and couldn't have provided a better cover if Luke had been designing it himself. The librarian's attention was immediately homed in on them, undoubtedly because the older man didn't want to have to clean up whatever the kids dug out right before closing.

Still, finding a place to hide where he wouldn't find them wouldn't be easy. Luke started scoping it out. He was back in the nonfiction section when Claire found him and motioned for him to follow.

"I can't believe it's still here," she whispered.

"What?"

She didn't answer, just gestured for him to keep following as they took a back aisle toward the children and teens section. The librarian was busy checking out the books for the mom and kids.

"Here." She walked over to a display that took up the entire back corner of the room. Worldwide scenes lit up the front, telling kids that reading could take them wherever they wanted to go.

"It's really nice." Luke didn't know what more to say. He vaguely remembered the display from their time here.

She walked over to the side of the display. "It's also still got a false back…"

"What?"

Claire pulled the back of the display from the side

it should've been attached to. Sure enough, it created an opening big enough to slip into.

An announcement came over the speaker that the library was closing in five minutes.

"Is it big enough for both of us?" he asked.

She nodded. "As long as you're not claustrophobic."

"Closed-in spaces aren't my favorite, but I'll manage."

He followed her as she slipped inside, then pulled the back panel into its rightful place.

It was definitely tight between the two of them and Khan's backpack. But claustrophobia was the last thing Luke was thinking about.

How could he when Claire's body was pressed up against him from head to toe?

"Hi," he whispered.

Her head dropped against his chest. "Fancy meeting you here. This space seemed a lot bigger when I hid here as a kid."

He put his hands on her hips. "You doing okay?"

He pulled her closer when she slid her arms around her waist. "Yeah."

They fell quiet, both smiling as they heard the librarian sing Broadway show tunes as he went about his closing duties. A few minutes later, when they heard everything switch off, Luke knew they were probably in the clear.

"Do you think it's safe to leave?" she whispered.

"I think we better stay in here a few more minutes."

A plan that had nothing to do with the librarian

and everything to do with him tilting up her face and bringing his lips down to hers.

He kept the kiss gentle and lazy, giving her plenty of opportunity to pull away if she wanted, and it wasn't long before he could feel her fingertips pushing against his back, bringing him *closer*, not away.

She wanted him, but it couldn't possibly be as much as he wanted her. He could stay here for hours and worship the generous curves of her mouth.

And that was nothing compared to what he'd like to do to the rest of her body.

But he forced himself to ease back. This wasn't the time or place for all the things he wanted to do to her, wanted them to do to each other.

He tilted his forehead against hers. They were both breathing heavily. "As much as I want to continue, we should save this for another time…"

"Yeah, you're right."

Khan meowed softly as if to offer his agreement, too. They both chuckled.

"Do you think it's safe to come out now?" she whispered.

"Yes." Luke turned so he could edge the back of the display open again. It was dim in the library. "Stay here while I double-check."

It didn't take long to confirm the building was empty. He returned to Claire and helped her out from the display.

She immediately set the backpack down so she could let the cat, literally, out of the bag. Khan stretched and walked around as if he owned the place.

"Okay, what do you need?" he asked.

"The computer lab. I'll hack into the statewide system so it hides where we are, then I will need to backdoor into Passage Digital." She began walking toward the lab.

"Stay away from the windows." It was dim in here, but not completely dark. They couldn't take a chance on being spotted by someone out walking their dog.

"Okay."

She chose the computer station in the back corner of the lab, fired it up, and started typing right away. There was no hesitation whatsoever.

"First, I have to bypass their password system."

He watched from over her shoulder. "How long will that take?"

"Already done it." Pleasure filled her voice. She was in her happy place.

"Already?" It took him longer than that to remember his own password most days.

She seemed not to hear him. With Khan at her feet, she was completely focused on the task at hand. He respected that kind of concentration and left her to it.

He moved back out of the computer lab and into the main section of the library, walking over to the side of a window and peeking out. Nothing out of the ordinary was happening in the empty parking lot. A glance out a window on the other side of the building, looking out into a playground and other buildings, resulted in the same.

This place brought back some good feelings for him. There weren't a lot in his earlier years. His life hadn't been too traumatic—nothing like what his brothers Chance or Brax went through—just a lot of hunger, combined with kicks and hits and well-placed bruises.

Life with the Pattersons had changed all that. Which reminded him that he needed to call his brothers.

He used his burner phone to dial Brax's cell number.

"Brax Patterson." Brax's voice was tense.

"It's me."

His brother let out a long exhale. "You all right? We saw the news."

"Yeah. We're both still alive." Luke leaned around a shelf to check on Claire. She typed away with laser focus, though her brown wig was askew.

"We've been waiting for you to call. The cops came by looking for you."

Even though it was news he'd expected, it still made Luke tense. "What did you say?"

"Exactly what you did. That you were away on a fishing trip. We even showed them the text."

"Did it throw them off?"

"They were still suspicious. Weston had a tail on him when he went out today. Where are you?"

"Somewhere that Claire can get the info she needs to clear her name." He lowered his voice. "She witnessed the murder of a coworker at Passage Digital. Now the CEO is trying to frame her for it. He's using all his political connections to bring her down hard."

Brax cursed sharply.

"Yeah, my feelings exactly."

"How can she prove her innocence?"

"Ballard isn't only guilty of murder. He's trying to use some app to illegally collect data on minors to be stored and used later—think access to bank accounts and private identity when the kids come of age."

Brax cursed again.

"She has proof of that on a drive," Luke continued. "But it's only readable through some proprietary software at Passage, so she's trying to hack her way into that. Once she can prove Ballard is guilty of identity theft, she'll be able to go to the police and show that he was using her as a scapegoat."

"What about the murder?"

"She's got video footage of it stuffed into the Passage Digital intraweb. She can't access it from outside, but if they arrest Ballard and let her into Passage, she'll be able to access it."

"Sounds like she's some sort of computer genius."

Pride filled Luke. "Exactly."

"How long will that take for her to get what she needs?"

"A few hours maybe. Hard to say." He rubbed the back of his neck. He didn't like the thought of being in one spot for so long, but there was no way around it. "Listen, once she gets what she needs, I need you to get Weston to meet Rick and arrange for us to come in tomorrow."

"Okay."

"Go see him face-to-face. Calling is too danger-ous," Luke warned. "Rick left his office to use a pay phone earlier to call me. He thinks this whole search for Claire smells rotten."

"That's because it is. We'll take care of it. You worry about everything on your end. I'll contact you in a few hours."

"Thanks, Brax." Some of the tension left his shoulders. He could always count on his family to come through.

Hanging up, Luke pulled one of the granola bars he'd picked up at the supermarket from his pocket and went back to the computer lab.

Claire was hunched forward, her face inches from the screen. "Dumb general user interface... So unprofessional..."

"Hey." He leaned against the wall next to the computer. "Time to eat something."

Her gaze remained fixed on the computer. "I'm not hungry."

"You need to keep your energy up. It's a stressful situation. You're burning more calories than you realize."

She extended a hand in his general direction but missed the granola bar by about a foot.

Chuckling, he slipped the bar into her palm. She promptly slapped it on the table next to the keyboard.

"You need to put it in your mouth for the eating thing to work." He crouched beside her and opened the wrapper. He took her hand off the keyboard and put the granola bar in it.

He stood back up when she gnawed on the snack with one hand still typing. Khan stretched out under the desk, waving a paw in the air. They were both in their zones, with only Luke left with nothing to do.

But he could do what he'd done for Claire even when they were kids—he would look out for her.

Leaving them at the desk, he walked to the other end of the library and back. He constantly kept diligent watch out various windows in between checking on her.

An hour went by.

Then another.

Then another.

By the time five had passed, and it was closer to dawn than sunset, he was starting to feel itchy. They'd been here too long. His instincts were starting to holler at him.

He wanted to give her as much time as possible, but time was running out.

"That's right…" she mumbled, as wide-awake as she'd been when they stepped into the library. "What do you think of that, Khan?"

He smirked from his perch near the periodicals. She'd been talking to the cat all night, and it made her even cuter.

But then she stiffened and stopped typing, the first time he'd seen her do that all night. "Uh-oh. That's not good."

He straightened and in a handful of strides, reached her chair. "What?" The coding stuff on her screen was all but a foreign language to him.

"I had to access the Passage Digital system remotely to be able to do what I need to."

He nodded, although he wasn't exactly certain what that meant.

"I knew they would see my intrusion into the system. I set it up so it looked like it was coming from one of the remote offices in Canada—nothing they'd deem too suspicious, just someone working late."

"What was the *uh-oh* about?"

"A few minutes ago, I thought maybe they'd caught me. An extra firewall went up."

"And that's bad?"

"Yeah, but expected. I was about to work my way around it, but then it dropped on its own."

"Why would it do that?"

She looked at him. "I'd like to say it's because the system doesn't see what I'm doing as a threat. But—"

"But it's more likely they're trying to keep you online," he finished for her.

She nodded. "Yes."

"How much more time do you need?"

"An hour. Maybe two. This is the most critical time."

"That's too long. Can you get any info at all in a shorter amount of time?"

"Maybe. It'll be a smash-and-grab, but it might work." She immediately started typing again; if possible, her fingers flew faster than they had been before.

He went back to the windows.

If they wanted to keep Claire online, it was because they were trying to track her.

He'd give her twenty more minutes, tops. After that, they had to go. It would no longer be safe here.

But less than a minute went by before one of the shadows out near the parking lot caught his attention. It was different than it had been before. Three hours of watching out these windows had ingrained the specifics of these shadows into his brain.

Sure enough, a few moments later, someone darted across the edge of the parking lot, moving from shadow to shadow to the side of the library. The only gleam that gave him away was when the moonlight reflected for a split second off the gun in his hand.

They didn't have twenty minutes.

"Claire," he said, raising his voice, "pack it up. We've got to go right now."

Chapter Ten

She didn't look up from her screen. "I'm almost done. Maybe thirty minutes."

They barely had thirty seconds, forget thirty minutes. "Now, Kitten."

She still didn't stop typing. "Really, I only need—"

Her protest morphed into a yelp as he wrapped an arm around her waist and lifted her from the seat.

"Ballard has been keeping you online to give his men time to get here. They're outside. We've got to go."

He set her down and she spun to face him. "What?"

"Ballard's men. Outside. I think that's what the firewall reversing was all about. They traced you here, and they're probably going to kill you."

He pulled open the backpack and shoved it into her hands. Khan bristled at the sight of the bag but allowed himself to be put inside. Luke zipped it almost the entire way, then loosened the straps and put it on his shoulders. He'd be able to run faster with it.

"We need to go out the employee exit." Taking Claire's hand, he rushed with her along the back wall.

At the door, they kept to the side as he looked out the window.

Damn it. Luke spotted two men before pulling his head back. Ballard's men had the library surrounded and it wouldn't be long before they breached the building.

He cursed under his breath. There would be no quick getaway.

"What?" she whispered.

"They've got us surrounded. They're covering both doors."

"What are we going to do?"

His mind raced. They needed a distraction. Calling the police wasn't an option, but…

He pulled the burner out of his pocket and dialed.

"9-1-1," the dispatcher answered, "what's your emergency?"

Luke took a couple of shallow breaths to make himself sound more panicked. "The Wars Hill library is on fire. Oh my gosh, it's spreading so fast. Please hurry." He hung up before the dispatcher could ask any further questions.

Claire's eyes widened. "Are we going to start a fire?"

"No, but the fire trucks and paramedics will be here soon. Hopefully, that'll chase off Ballard's men and we'll get away in the confusion."

She looked skeptical, and he couldn't blame her. He fought back a tiny smile at the sight of her. Her brown wig had gotten pretty twisted and wisps of blond hair kissed the corners of her face. Once again, she looked like the little girl he'd known.

Little girl or grown woman, there was no way in hell he was letting Ballard's men get her.

The sound of a lock breaking and the emergency alarm being smashed to eliminate the noise echoed through the library. Luke grabbed her hand and pulled her back to the display in the children's section.

They barely made it inside before they heard voices.

"Check every aisle," a man called. "They're in here somewhere."

Luke pulled Claire's stiff form against him. He cocked his head, trying to figure out exactly how many men there were as they talked. Three? Four?

He was a good shot, but he wouldn't have much chance at getting them all before they got shots off themselves.

A ringing phone only a few feet away from the display made Claire jerk. Luke tugged her closer to him, wrapping his fingers around her nape, massaging gently. It was over for them if she had some sort of panic attack now.

"Hello?" one of the men answered. Brief silence followed. "Damn it. We haven't found them. Maybe they got out before we got here, but there's not going to be enough time for a thorough search." More silence. "Yes, sir."

The man yelled louder, "Fire department is en route thanks to a 9-1-1 call. ETA less than five."

"Bathrooms and employee rooms are clear," another voice responded from farther away. "No sign of them."

"We don't have enough time to search thoroughly. But we'll give the fire department a real fire to fight and cover the exits. There's a gas canister in the van. Have Brickman bring it in. Hurry."

Damn it, Luke had handed the bad guys exactly what they needed by placing that emergency call.

The best bet was still to stay put. Getting out in the chaos of the fire would give them a better chance of survival than facing their guns.

The smell of gas a minute later had Luke reconsidering that notion. Then the pungent smell of smoke.

"Make sure we've got both doors covered. We'll get them running out or when the fire department brings out their charred bodies." The voices faded as the smell of smoke grew stronger.

"What do we do?" Claire's pitch was high and her breathing was way too rapid.

"It's okay," he whispered. "Just wait a minute." They had to make sure no one was still inside the building.

Their best bet was to stay alive until the firefighters arrived, and then they could get out with them. More witnesses equaled more protection.

But that was easier said than done. The smoke invading the air caused all his survival instincts to kick into overdrive. His feet ached to run.

"Luke?"

"They have to be gone by now. We're going to keep low and crawl out." He pushed aside the display so he could crawl out.

They moved on their hands and knees, Khan meowing pathetically from the bag slung over his back.

"Which door are we using?" She coughed into her hand.

"We have to stay here and wait for the fire department."

He had to give her credit; she didn't give in to hysteria. "Will we make it that long?"

"We have to. If we go out either door now," he said, "they'll shoot us on sight."

She was right, the fire was spreading too fast for them to be able to breathe by the time the fire department arrived, even if it was just a couple of minutes. This place was an arsonist's dream.

They both had pulled their shirts to cover their mouths, but even low to the ground, the smoke was getting thicker. The heat from the burning books surrounded them from all directions.

They were going to have to exit. Take their chances.

"We're going to go out the front door." He put his lips right next to her ear so she could hear him. "You stay behind me and then run for the nearest emergency worker."

Her whole body was shaking. "They'll shoot. They'll shoot you first to get to me."

"It's a chance we'll have to take. They're covering the doors, but we can't stay in here."

Her eyes grew larger. "Wait. I have an idea. Follow me."

She scurried off toward the back of the building. He almost stopped her—going out the front where there were potentially more people was probably a better plan. But then she turned toward the western end of the building.

The bathrooms. That might buy them a little bit of time, but it might trap them.

He grabbed her ankle where she crawled in front of him. She turned. "The bathrooms might trap us," he yelled to be heard over the fire.

She yelled something back, but he could only make out one word, but it was the most important one.

Window.

They made it inside, the thinner smoke allowing them to stand and breathe a little easier. Luke unzipped the backpack and let Khan out, grabbing the clothing that had lined the bottom and stuffing it in the crack at the door. It would buy them a little more time.

"There's a window in the storage closet." She pointed at a closed door. "I used it once when I was maxed out on my book checkouts but had another story I really wanted to read. But I returned it."

Even in the middle of all this, she actually looked embarrassed that she'd stolen a book.

Luke didn't waste any time; he moved to the door and when he found it locked, he kicked it near the knob.

One look at the window had him swallowing a curse. He was sure eleven-year-old Claire had made it through with her stolen book. Adult Claire was going to be a tighter fit, but she would make it. *Him?*

Claire chewed her bottom lip. "Wow. That's a lot smaller than I remember…"

"You'll fit."

"What about you?"

"I'll fit, too."

He grabbed the large flashlight in the corner of the closet and wrapped it in a shirt, using it to break the window as quietly as possible. Ballard's men probably wouldn't be looking for them in this direction, but there was no point in drawing their attention.

It broke with the second hit and he cleared the glass out as much as possible. "You need to go first. I'll hoist you up. Watch the edges."

When he whirled around, she was holding Khan out to him.

Of course she was.

"Come on, cat." Khan knew what to do and scurried through the window to safety. There were no sounds from the outside, a good sign.

He turned back to Claire, linking his hands together so she could step into them. It took barely any effort to hoist her up, and she slid through the opening without difficulty.

His turn.

Grabbing hold of the window's bottom frame, he pulled himself up. Little bits of glass pricked his palms, but he ignored the pain and wiggled into the window until his shoulders got stuck.

Damn it.

He had to ease himself back into the closet to come at the window from another angle. The smoke was getting bad. If he couldn't make it through, he might not be getting out of this building at all.

He pulled himself up again, twisting to make himself as narrow as possible through the shoulders. He bit back a curse at the sharp pain ripping through his shirt and into his flesh—a piece of glass that had shifted. There was nowhere to get away from it, so he pulled his shoulders the rest of the way through, gritting his teeth at the burn.

Once his shoulders were out, the rest was slightly easier. Twisting again, he used the wall to give himself leverage. By the time he was all the way out, he could feel the blood soaking his shirt and was barely able to keep from coughing from the smoke inhalation.

He sucked in a deep breath. There would be time later to rest and worry about his wound. Right now, he needed to get them out of here. "Let's head for the bushes, Kitten."

When there was no response, he looked in both directions but didn't see any sign of Claire. Ignoring his screaming shoulder, he moved to rise.

And stopped at a voice that definitely wasn't Claire's.

"Don't move and keep your hands where I can see them."

Chapter Eleven

Luke's gun was tucked in the back waistband of his jeans. This guy would definitely get a shot off if he went for it, especially slowed down by his shoulder.

He raised his hands. "Easy."

"Where's the woman?" The man took a step closer.

Luke fought not to let his relief be seen. If they were still looking for Claire, then that meant they didn't have her. Yet.

"What woman?" Maybe feigning innocence would buy him some time.

The guy stepped closer. "You know who I'm talking about."

"I don't know who you're talking about. I just fell asleep in the library. The place is on fire, man."

He tried to check his peripheral vision for any sign of Claire. Was she safe? She wouldn't have just left him there. Maybe she'd run off after Khan.

The guy's eyes narrowed. "I don't know who you are or how you got involved with her, but she's guilty of murder. If you tell me where she is, we'll make sure she's brought to justice before she hurts anyone else. You don't have to get hurt. Nobody else needs to get hurt."

The guy kept his weapon steady and trained on Luke. He was definitely a professional.

"I don't know who or what you're talking about." Luke continued his charade, spoke slowly and kept his hands up. "I just want to get away from this burning building."

"If you don't know who or where she is, then you're not of any use to us. Might as well get rid of you now."

So much for them being the good guys.

The man kept his gun trained on Luke as he brought his walkie-talkie up with his other hand. "This is Brickman. Tell Kenneth I've got—"

With a sickening thud, Brickman crumpled. His gun hit the ground, followed by his face.

Right behind where he'd just been standing, Claire stood, holding up the wooden skateboard she'd just used to clobber the guy. "Is he dead?" Poking his head around Claire's legs, Khan meowed.

Luke hauled himself to his feet, pain shooting through his shoulder. "No. You knocked him out." He nudged Brickman with his foot just to make sure. The jerk groaned incoherently.

"Are you okay?" She dropped the skateboard. "I heard him coming around the corner and had to hide. I didn't just leave you."

He forced a smile. "I never thought that. You did the smart thing. Now we need to get out of here before they come looking for Brickman."

He grabbed her hand and began to pull her toward

the bushes. She immediately yanked her hand free. "Luke. Oh my gosh. You're covered in blood!"

He grimaced. "I cut my shoulder going through the window. I'm okay. We've got to go."

A blue light flashed across Claire's face from a police car. One vehicle was just pulling into the library's front parking lot, but the sirens screaming through the night promised that more first responders were on their way.

She was still staring at his shoulder. "You're hurt bad," she whispered.

He would have to suck it up—Ballard's men were everywhere. "Survive now. Tend to the wounds later."

She nodded. Taking her hand with his good one, they darted for the few trees near the playground on the side of the blazing building. Khan stayed right with them.

They needed to get away from here.

"I don't think we can get directly to the truck," he muttered with a curse. There were too many of Ballard's men and now too many first responders.

"We should go that way." She pointed toward the back parking lot. "That leads farther into town, which means more places to hide."

He glanced back at the line of tall, manicured bushes behind the library's back lot. It would provide a perfect escape, but he was less familiar with that area and it was in the opposite direction of the truck. "Are you sure?"

She nodded. "Yes. I came back to this area for my

last foster family in high school. We can hide until it's clear, then circle back."

More lights, both red and blue, flashed against the greenery. The fire department had arrived out front.

But another cop car had pulled up in the back lot. Damn it. They'd have to be doubly careful now—avoiding Ballard's men and the police.

They crept along, staying in the shadows. Organized chaos was evident in the front with the fire department concentrating on the burning building. Hopefully nobody would be paying much attention back here.

He nudged Claire forward through a break in the bushes. Turning sideways to fit, he scooted through, wincing when the sharp leaves scraped his shoulder.

Claire's gasp turned his blood cold.

One of Ballard's men was there waiting, his weapon drawn.

The man gave them a cocky smile. "I knew you two were still around here somewhere. Count yourself lucky. Bullet is a better way to die than fire."

A helpless rage swallowed Luke. He wouldn't even be able to get in front of Claire to shield her.

"Freeze!"

The command came from the parking lot a few yards to the side of Ballard's man. He kept his gun trained on Claire as he tilted his head to the side to talk to the cop.

"Officer— Thank goodness! I've got that fugitive that's been on the TV. She has a gun, be careful!"

Then, without hesitation, Ballard's man spun and shot the cop.

Luke leaped for the guy, pushing Claire out of the way. The man had shot that cop and there was no doubt that Luke and Claire were next on his list.

The sharp edge of his palm came down hard on the inside of the man's elbow. The stranger's hold slackened and the gun fell to the ground.

He was quick, though. Trained. A fist came flying toward Luke's face.

A swift block and ignoring the screaming pain from his shoulder, Luke nailed his opponent with an uppercut. The man staggered back. Luke followed, hitting him with a right hook.

The punches had the intended effect—Ballard's man hit the ground, knocked out cold.

But the fight had taken a toll on Luke, too. Hot, sticky blood dripped down his hand. It had been a bad idea to strike with that arm. He drew a deep breath, trying to stop his head from spinning. A tug on his hand brought him back to his senses.

Claire.

"Are you okay?"

"Yeah." No. He needed to sit down. Needed to get this bleeding under control. Needed to take a moment and regroup.

And maybe he would've if it was just him on his own. But he couldn't. He had to get Claire to safety.

"Is that policeman…?"

"Dead? I don't know. But we can't wait and help him, not if we want to get away."

He took out his burner phone. It wouldn't be much use any longer anyway, now that he'd used it to call Brax. He dialed 9-1-1 again. As soon as the responder picked up, he spoke.

"Officer down behind the Wars Hill library. He's been shot."

He ended the call immediately before the dispatcher could ask questions and grabbed Claire's hand. It would be only moments before the 9-1-1 dispatch notified the police already on the scene here. Calling might have been a mistake, but if there was anything that could be done to save that cop, Luke had to take that chance. Hopefully, it would be enough.

But he and Claire had to get out *now*.

They moved slower along the bushes toward the street on the east side of the building. Luke didn't want to take a chance on stumbling into another one of Ballard's men. The odds of him winning a second fight in his shape were slim.

And Claire would be unprotected.

But if they kept moving this slowly, they might get caught anyway. Luke was slowing them down. Running was not an option. The way the night was spinning, fast *walking* was barely an option.

He squeezed her hand as they passed by the alleyway. They just needed to make it a few more blocks.

But he wasn't sure he was going to be able to.

"You need to run. Leave me behind. Get farther into the main section of town. You know your way around, you can hide."

"No. I'm not leaving you."

"You have to. I don't think I'm going to make it much farther."

They only needed to go another mile or so, but that seemed impossible. Ten more steps seemed impossible.

She slipped her arm around his waist, tucking herself under his good shoulder. "Lean on me. Just take it one step at a time."

"Go without me."

"You're wasting time and energy arguing, Patterson. I'm not leaving you, so we either both stay here or we both go."

He almost smiled at her bossy tone and took a step forward. And another.

Praying none of Ballard's men would find them, he kept moving forward. Left down a dark block. Right down a second alleyway. His legs weakened. His arm burned like hell. He couldn't stop, though. Wouldn't let anything happen to Claire. *Kitten.*

Were they far enough? He had no idea where they were—walking along some empty street. Had no idea how much time had passed since they left the library. Five minutes? An hour? Ten years?

He had to stop. He leaned heavily with his good shoulder against a parked semitruck that shielded them from anyone on the street.

"You keep going." The words sounded raspy, breathless, not like his voice at all.

She ignored his statement, tentatively touched his shoulder, making him wince. "It looks bad."

"It's okay." A lie, but what else could he say?

All he needed was a few minutes. A place to rest until he regained his strength.

He couldn't contact his brothers—he'd had to dump the burner phone. They couldn't make it back to the truck.

Think, Luke. Think.

He couldn't. He slid to the ground.

It felt so damn good to sit. He closed his eyes. One second of rest. Maybe two…

Something fluffy brushed against his chest. Khan's tail.

Good doggy.

"Bandage it… Shirt is dirty…"

Claire's voice went in and out, impossible to follow.

"We need to go." Planting his palm against the cold metal of the truck, he pushed himself to standing.

And promptly collapsed toward the concrete, the world spinning uncontrollably around him.

Chapter Twelve

"Luke!" Claire caught him before he hit the ground.

His weight bowed her over. Using all her strength, she got him back to sitting, his back propped against the truck.

The streetlight at the end of the block shone on his shoulder. The cut gleamed, shiny and dark.

She'd thought about putting her shirt on the wound, but it had gotten so dirty from crawling out the window, it would probably cause infection.

His head lolled to the side. "Kitten."

Khan spun in a circle, his dance move when anxious. He could tell something was wrong.

A ball formed in Claire's throat. She had to get Luke somewhere safe. She hadn't seen any sign of Ballard's men in the last thirty minutes, but that didn't mean they weren't still searching for them.

She was going to have to take Luke to the hospital, and hope nobody would come looking for them.

She trailed her fingers through his hair, then cupped his cheeks. "Luke. I need you to listen to me, okay?"

His brown eyes blinked open at her. They were glazed with pain, but he was still with her.

"We need to get you to a hospital."

"No. Find us too easy."

"We have to. You need stitches."

He grabbed her wrist where she cupped his face. "No. Too dangerous. Promise."

Damn it. He was probably right, but she had to do something. Get him somewhere they were inside and safe. They didn't have enough money left for another hotel—and Ballard would undoubtedly be searching any nearby establishments for check-ins anyway.

All right, no hospital. No doc-in-a-box, either. They would want names, insurance info, stuff that went into a computer and would enable Ballard to find them.

Khan rubbed up against her. "Where would you want to go if you were hurt, Khan?"

A vet. Of course. That's it!

"You're a genius, Khan."

The cat continued to prance around like he was well aware of the fact that he was amazing.

She'd spent a lot of time in the neighborhood they were in. After leaving Skyline Park, the first foster family she'd gone to had lived only a couple miles from here.

And then, the summer after high school, she'd worked at the independent vet just up the block. It had been one of the happiest times of her life—waking up early and spending her days with animals.

The first time she'd seen a Maine coon in person

was when someone brought theirs in with a hurt paw. She'd fallen in love with the breed right away and started saving that night in order to buy her own one day.

"Luke. Listen." She bowed her head so they were eye to eye again. "There's a vet's office near here. It has an apartment garage we might be able to get into. It's only a couple of blocks away. Can you walk that far?"

For a second she thought he was unconscious again, but finally, he nodded gingerly. "Yeah."

"Great." Scooping a hand under his good arm, she helped him stand.

Years had passed and she didn't even know if Dr. McGraw's practice was still open. Back when she worked there, he'd converted the space above the detached garage into a studio apartment. On nights when he worked overtime and was too tired to commute home, he stayed there. But that had rarely happened on weekends. He'd wanted to be home with his wife because the grandkids came over.

They walked slowly in the correct direction, her carrying as much of his weight as possible.

This plan had a lot of unknown variables. She prayed it would work, because otherwise, she didn't know what she was going to do.

Khan circled them as they walked, darting ahead and coming back to check on their progress. It was slow going, and every time headlights appeared, they ducked behind the nearest vehicle or trash can.

They turned a corner and she glanced behind her

and saw the orange of the fire in the distance. The sight made Claire's chest ache. Her beloved childhood safe haven was gone.

Ballard's men may have been the ones who'd started the fire, but Claire had been the one who led them to that building. And now Luke had been hurt because of her.

She pushed the feelings down. Right now she had to focus on getting them somewhere safe. Luke's wound seemed to have stopped bleeding. He was conscious but still so very weak. He'd always taken care of her, and now it was time for her to do the same for him.

It was dark in the veterinary clinic. It sat next to a house that had been renovated into a beauty salon, across the street from a local hardware store. Luke was on the last of his reserves as they made it down the narrow drive between the salon and the clinic to the garage in the back.

She let out a sigh of relief when there were no lights on in the garage or the studio apartment that rested above it.

She set Luke at the bottom of the wooden steps that went up the side of the garage.

"I'll be right back," she whispered to Luke as he slumped on the stairs. Khan sat down at his feet.

"I'm coming with." Luke grabbed hold of the weathered railing and started to pull himself up. "Not…leaving you."

"No, you're staying." She put a hand on his chest,

and he stilled. "I'll be right back. I can move faster without you."

A quick kiss to his lips revealed they were cold. Not good. They had to get him inside pronto. The fact that he didn't argue further just proved that point.

She took the steps two at a time. Cupping her hands around her eyes, she pressed against the window on the door and peered into the apartment.

The vague shapes of furniture rose from the dark room. She didn't see any people—just a lot more boxes than had been around when she worked there.

She reached over to the light fixture and ran her fingers under the edge, letting out a shuddery sigh of relief when she found the key in the same place Dr. McGraw had always kept it.

With shaking hands, she unlocked the door and let it swing open, listening for any sounds before stepping inside.

"Hello?" Nothing. She went in and looked around. It was empty. Thank God. She turned and hurried back down the steps.

Khan was still standing guard over Luke. She wrapped her arm around his torso while he held on to her shoulder. "Come on, it's empty." They slowly made their way up the stairs. "And tomorrow is Sunday. If Dr. McGraw didn't spend tonight here, he won't come in tomorrow."

At least, she hoped that was still true. If not, the police would just have to add breaking and entering to their list of reasons to arrest her.

The studio apartment wasn't much. Boxes and supplies took up one entire wall. There was a small full bed in one corner and a love seat in front of the TV in the middle. She helped Luke sit on the carpet, leaning his good side against the couch so he wouldn't get blood on it. Khan started his rounds, sniffing the corners of the room, while Claire closed all the blinds.

Once she was confident no light would escape the apartment and give away their presence, she switched on a standing lamp. The paleness of Luke's face was striking, made even more prominent by the dark circles under his eyes.

"We need to get your shirt off so I can see the cut." Sitting on her knees next to him, she helped remove it. He winced when he had to move his hurt arm but didn't make a peep.

His shirt was completely ruined and most of his back was covered in blood. She gasped when she saw the cut. It wasn't very deep, but it was long and had to be painful. "Luke, you need stitches."

"No." His voice was thin, weak. "They'd put my name in a computer. Ballard would have us in thirty minutes."

"Luke…" An invisible weight pressed against her throat and chest. He was too big for her to force to a medical facility.

She gritted her teeth, hating that it was her situation that was causing him literal physical pain right now. Her situation that meant he couldn't get the help he needed.

"Let me see what I can find."

Rooting around in the cabinet under the sink, she

found a fully stocked first aid kit, as well as some protein bars and nutrition drinks. Those would help his body begin to replenish everything it had expended.

When she returned, Khan had stopped his exploring and sat next to Luke, licking his hand.

She opened a drink and handed it to him before settling cross-legged behind him. She pressed a clean piece of gauze to the cut but fresh blood quickly seeped through.

She changed out the gauze and applied pressure the best she could as he finished one nutrition drink and she handed him another one.

"How's it looking back there?"

He finally sounded like Luke again, like he wasn't about to keel over. But she still had to tell him.

"It looks like this gauze isn't enough. You need stitches. Really, Luke."

"Okay."

"We can go to the hospital?"

"No, you're going to use that suture kit over there and do it yourself."

She looked over to where he was pointing, and sure enough, resting on one of the boxes of supplies was a sealed suture kit for the clinic.

She shook her head frantically and scooted back from him. "No, I can't do that. I don't know how to give someone stitches." She was glad for the nutrition drinks and that a chance to rest had him feeling better, but this was crazy.

"When you worked here at the vet clinic, did you ever see them stitch up an animal?"

"Sure, a lot."

"It's the same concept. Basically, just sewing. I had to do it once in the army when our medic got injured while we are on a mission. He talked me through it. I can talk you through this."

"If you're Hannibal Lecter," she muttered.

He chuckled. "That was the other guy. Hannibal just ate them." He turned so he was facing her more fully. "I know this is gross, but it's our best bet."

"It's not that it's gross…" she whispered. "It's going to hurt you."

He leaned over and kissed her tenderly, his full lips soft against hers. "I'll be okay, I promise."

"I don't know if I can do this."

"You can, Kitten. I trust you."

Chapter Thirteen

Her hands shook as she got the kit and cleaned out his wound. She knew it had to hurt every time the needle pierced his skin—it hurt her just to see it—but he never gave her any indication of distress.

"How did you end up working here?" he asked when she let out a distressed breath at the start of the third stitch.

"It was the summer after my freshman year in college. The Romeros, my last foster family, were nice enough to let me come back and live with them after my first year at school. They didn't live too far from here, so it was a fun and convenient summer job."

She winced as the needle pierced his skin again and she pulled the string to pull the edges of skin together, then tied it up with a knot.

"That's good. My parents, Sheila and Clinton Patterson, are big fighters for older-age adoption and foster. One of their biggest causes was that kids needed a family, even after they aged out of the system. They still need somewhere to go when they're young adults… The need for a support network doesn't change just because you turn eighteen."

"Yeah. The Romeros were good. I haven't talked to them in the while. I probably should."

She started another stitch.

"So, you liked working here?"

"Absolutely. The first time I ever saw a Maine coon was here. I even thought I might want to be a vet for a while, but I knew that would take a lot of schooling. Plus, I was already really good at computers."

"Chance and I both went into the army straight out of high school. Brax and Weston went on to college."

"No college for you?"

"I finished my associate's degree in business, but I'm not a huge fan of sitting in classrooms. I'd rather be out crawling through burning buildings and dodging bullets."

She laughed as she finished another stitch.

"The army gave me a purpose. I was always pretty physically strong and had good hand-eye coordination and spatial awareness. I was good at reading people and recognizing threats. It would've made a good skill set for working for someone like Ballard, or the equivalent. Being in the service helped me hone a sense of honor. Clarified the path that Clinton and Sheila started me on. I got out with the skills and purpose I needed to start San Antonio Security with my brothers."

"And you like it? It's done well?"

"Being in business with family always has its pros and cons. For example, none of us like to do paperwork and this month it's my turn. I'd honestly rather sit here and let you do this to me for the rest of the month than have to do all the filing that's waiting for me at my desk. So if we get this murder charge cleared up, we might have to rob a bank or something just so I don't have to go back to the office." She laughed again and finished another stitch.

"Maybe that's how I'll have to pay you back for helping me—paperwork."

"I wouldn't wish that on my worst enemy. Well, maybe I'd wish it on Ballard. Except for what has happened over the last few days, have you liked working at Passage Digital?"

He was helping her, she realized. In the only way he could.

"Thank you."

"For what?" he asked. "Asking about your job?"

"I know what you're doing…you're distracting me. Given the circumstances, it should be the other way around. So, thank you."

"I do want to know about your job. About you. I thought about you all the time, Kitten. I can't tell you how many times I thought about using San Antonio Security's resources to find you, check up on you, but I didn't want to invade your privacy like that."

"I've had a pretty uneventful life up until a couple of weeks ago. I liked working at Passage. Mostly because people there left me alone, as pathetic as that sounds."

He chuckled. "You've never been a people person."

"Nope, that didn't change about me. My job was…a

job. I went in, I did it, and I was good at it. I understand computers and they don't exhaust me. My team
leader, Julia—" Claire had to swallow back tears. "She
and I weren't really friends, but she was nice to me.
She knew I worked best alone, so she rarely put me
on group projects."

"I'm sorry, Kitten. Friendships come in all different
shapes and sizes. Yours may not have been a traditional
one, but she was still your friend."

"Yeah." She never thought of it that way, but it
was true.

"We're going to make sure Ballard pays for what
he has done."

Claire wasn't so sure. Ballard seemed to have the
upper hand and now he was going to be looking any
time she tried to access Digital Passage remotely.

She finished another stitch. She had to focus on
what was in front of her; looking at the big picture
was just going to overwhelm her. That was how she
worked a computer problem, and it was how she
needed to work this situation.

"How about your personal life? Ever been…mar-
ried or anything?"

"No. A couple of boyfriends in college, but nothing serious. Trust issues, people issues, you know
the deal. You?"

Her heart clenched as he waited so long, she was
afraid he wasn't going to answer.

"You and I are a lot alike in terms of people. I
don't necessarily avoid all contact with people, but

my brothers all know not to send me in with clients. I'm way too gruff."

"You're not too gruff with me."

"You're the exception, Kitten. You always have been. And no, there hasn't been anyone very serious for me, either."

She finished the last two stitches.

"You vaguely resemble Frankenstein's monster, but I think this will at least help it heal more quickly and keep out infection."

"Thank you."

She began cleaning up all her supplies on the table and put them in a trash bag. They'd have to take that out with them when they left in the morning.

"You got that because of me, so no thanks is necessary."

He moved in front of her and cupped her cheeks.

"I got that because Ballard is a lying murderous bastard, not because of you. Because of your bravery and grit, I'm safe here in this apartment. I'm stitched up and better able to help protect us if we need it. That is because of you. Not the other stuff." She didn't know if she believed that, but at least for the moment, they were safe.

He chugged down a third nutrition shake and helped her finish cleaning. They found a couple of cans of soup and some crackers and Luke made a meal of it. Now that Luke was looking much steadier on his feet and strong enough to take on the world again, she found it difficult to stop staring at his very well-developed and muscular chest. Eventually they would have to find a shirt for him to put on, but for now she would enjoy the view. Fortunately, he didn't seem to notice her embarrassed fascination, or if he did, he was too polite to tease her about it.

As a matter of fact, he may claim to be gruff, but he was charming and friendly to her despite her having tortured him for the past hour.

"I'm going to take a shower," she announced after they cleared away the few dishes they had used. They were trying to clean up any messes as they went, just in case they had to leave in a hurry.

"Good idea. I'll wash off the best I can after you."

He flipped on the TV as she headed for the bathroom, but she stopped, turning in horror when she heard her name on the news.

"Local police this evening are asking for special assistance to find Claire Wallace."

A picture of Claire filled the screen.

"Wallace was already wanted for questioning by the police for the murder of Julia Lindsey, a colleague and employee at Passage Digital. Now Wallace is wanted for the fire that destroyed Wars Hill library earlier this evening and for the shooting of a police officer. There is a reward for any information that leads to the capture of Wallace." A phone number and email address floated across her picture on the screen.

Claire couldn't stop the sob that escaped her. Luke was at her side in an instant. He reached out with the remote control and flipped the TV off.

"Hey." He reached out to pull her into his arms, but she stepped back.

"Hey," he said again. "This doesn't change anything. We're still going to figure out a way to clear your name."

She nodded blankly. But how? How were they going to clear her name? Ballard had all the advantages, especially now that the cops thought she was the one who had shot that officer.

"I'm going to take a shower."

She wasn't sure if she was relieved or disappointed when Luke let her go. Once in the bathroom, she pulled her clothes off but brought them with her into the shower.

She used the body wash to try to get rid of some of the smoky smell on her clothes, then rinsed them thoroughly. Then she scrubbed her body from head to toe until she was almost raw.

That got rid of the smoky smell, but it didn't change the fact that the situation had gotten even more dire. Who was she kidding? What were her real chances of being able to beat someone like Ballard? All she was doing now was dragging Luke into danger. He'd already been hurt because of it.

The towel was her only option while her clothes dried. She wrapped it around herself, thankful for once of her small stature since it covered enough of her to keep her decent.

Luke watched as she came out and sat on the bed, studying her with concern.

Certainly, he was not as distracted by the sight of some of her skin as she had been by his bare chest.

But what did she expect? Just because he'd been

nice to her and had kissed her a couple of times didn't mean he thought of her as anything more than just someone he used to know and was helping for old times' sake. Given the circumstances, she should be glad he was even willing to do that.

"At least I don't smell like a furnace anymore." She tried for a lighthearted laugh, but it came out sounding stilted at best.

He nodded. "I'm going to wash off as best I can without getting my stitches wet. Then we should probably try to catch a few hours of sleep before figuring out our next plan." She nodded and lay back. It was well after midnight and they could both use the rest.

Given everything, she should've been exhausted, but sleep wouldn't come. Still wrapped in the towel, she got under the covers hoping that would help, but it didn't. She just kept seeing the fire and Luke's wound and that guy with the gun.

It was a nightmare she couldn't wake up from.

"Whoa. Hey, Kitten, you're shaking."

Claire hadn't even been aware that Luke had gotten out of the shower or sat down on the bed next to her.

"I'm… I'm okay."

She wasn't okay. She very definitely wasn't okay.

"Hey. Hey, come here."

She didn't even think about resisting when he pulled her into his arms. He held her so close to him, his body absorbed her tremors until they finally stopped.

"I'm sorry. I'm acting like an idiot."

He kissed along her forehead, keeping her wrapped up against him. She couldn't remember ever feeling so secure.

"Don't say that. I've known guys in the Special Forces who would have crumbled much harder under the pressure you've been through. You're doing amazing."

"I just don't see how anything is ever going to be right again."

She felt his fingers stroke along the bare skin of her shoulder blades as he laid them back. The shiver that ran through her this time had nothing to do with despondency.

"We're going to figure this out. I know it seems hopeless right now, but I promise you, we are going to figure out a way to clear your name and make sure Ballard goes down."

He said it with such deep, gruff authority, it was impossible not to believe him. She lifted her head off his chest so she could see his eyes. He was so sexy.

"Thank you. For everything."

She leaned forward to give him a friendly kiss, but the moment she did, everything changed.

The kiss started soft but grew passionate and heated. This was what she wanted. She wanted to have this passion with him, even if it was only for tonight. She might have to make some hard choices to protect him in the morning, but for tonight, she wanted whatever she could get.

When she felt his hand tangle in her still-damp hair, pulling her closer, she knew Luke felt the same.

She gave herself over to the kiss, almost scrambling on top of him in an effort to get closer.

But then he stopped.

She was so wound up, she didn't even realize that he wasn't kissing her with the same abandon that she was kissing him. It wasn't until the hand that had been fisted in her hair loosened and he slid back that she became aware of it.

"Luke?"

"Kitten. You've been through so much. I'm not sure this is a good idea."

Claire felt like her insides were being turned to pieces of ice. "You don't want me? You don't think of me that way?"

"Are you kidding?" He slid his hand down and yanked her hips against his. "Believe me, I want you. But you've been through enough. I don't want you to feel pressured. I don't want this to be something you'll regret."

The ice inside her began to fall. He did want her. He was just so protective, always had been.

She reached up and scraped her fingers gently down his jaw, loving the feel of the stubble growing there.

"I want you. There may end up being a lot of things I regret, but this is definitely not one of them."

His brown eyes bored into hers. "Are you sure? I don't expect anything. You don't owe me any—"

She shut him up with a kiss. He probably still had another twenty minutes' worth of protective alpha male speech to give her.

But she knew that she wanted him.

He took the hint and stopped trying to talk her out of what they both desperately wanted. Their lips fused together in a duel, a battle in which both of them won.

Then, as he kissed down her body, moving away the towel as he went, it chased away all the thoughts of Ballard and death and the inescapable mess she was in.

All she could feel was Luke.

Chapter Fourteen

Luke woke up the next morning groggy, which was unusual for him. His life had never been one where deep sleep and waking up disoriented were leisures he could afford.

But clarity came when he realized Claire was not in the bed beside him. A quick glance at the bathroom and around this small studio space confirmed his worst fears.

She was gone.

Damn it. His body was tired from yesterday's trauma and then the three rounds of lovemaking with her last night. He hadn't been able to keep his hands off her. And he wouldn't trade a single second of it, except that it meant he hadn't woken up when she decided to sneak off.

Khan.

He saw the note on the small table at the same time he saw Khan stretch out by the door.

His heart sank as he read her words.

Dear Luke,
I couldn't stay. This was too dangerous for me to have involved you in—and now you've gotten hurt. I'm going to go to the police, tell them everything I know, and hope for the best. Maybe I can make them listen and give me a chance to prove my innocence. This lets me protect you for once. Please take care of Khan. I know you know how important he is to me. Thank you for last night. Thank you for everything, now and when we were kids.

Love,
Claire

Luke was already getting dressed, having to use one of the vet clinic polo shirts lying in a box since his was way too bloodied and he did not want to draw attention to himself. He grabbed Khan, knowing she'd never forgive him if something happened to the cat, and rushed out the door, praying he wasn't too late to stop her.

There might come a time when her only option was to go to the police and hope they could find one who was on the up-and-up and would listen to her, but that wasn't until they ran out of all their other options.

And it damn well wasn't going to be because she wanted to protect him.

The closest precinct was about a mile away. Luke didn't even bother trying to blend in with any sort of walk. There was no way he could blend in when carrying this giant cat anyway. He ran full out, ignoring the pain in his shoulder and the occasional cat claw hooked into his biceps. At least the cat wasn't fighting him and trying to get away.

"Good boy."

This thing really was more like a dog. Maybe he sensed his mistress was in trouble. "Not on my watch, buddy." It was early enough on a Sunday morning that there weren't many people out. All things considered, Luke made pretty good time. When he turned around the last corner that put the precinct in his sights, he let out a silent prayer.

Claire was standing just down the block from the station, pacing and talking to herself. *Thank God.*

Luke slowed to a walk; he definitely couldn't draw attention to himself now. He kept his eyes trained on Claire. There was no way he was going to let her go in there.

He had just found her again after all these years, and he couldn't lose her now.

He kept on the other side of the street from the precinct. She was so busy arguing with herself, preparing her statement or whatever she was doing, that she didn't even see them.

Even in this dire situation, Luke couldn't help but smile. This woman… She'd amazed him when they were kids, and she continued to do so now. Last night had just solidified that.

He crossed the street a little farther down from her so he was coming up behind her. Khan began to get a little restless in his arms as he saw Claire.

"I know, buddy. We're going to get her out of here."

Luke moved quietly up behind her and was able to see the two cops who walked out of the precinct and headed in her direction at the same time she did. She stiffened, and he knew she was about to make her move.

He dropped Khan and quickly stepped in front of her, blocking Claire from the cops' view.

He pulled her in for a hug. "Hi, honey," he said just loudly enough that the cops would be able to hear him but not so loud that it seemed unnatural. "Ready to go get our coffee?"

The officers never even slowed down, caught in their own conversation as they continued down the block.

Luke kept one arm around her and turned them to cross the street in the opposite direction of both the cops and the precinct.

"Did you get my note? I want to turn myself in."

He didn't stop walking and Khan stayed right at their feet. "That's exactly what Ballard is hoping you'll do. He's prepared for that. You can bet he has some sort of plan. You turning yourself in without proof in hand will be a death sentence."

She was still resisting. "You got hurt. You could've been killed. I meant what I said in the note."

He stopped walking so he could turn and face her eye-to-eye. He brought both hands up to cup her cheeks and ran his thumbs over her delicate cheekbones. "Kitten, you have no idea what it means to me that you want to protect me, but this is not the way to do it. We find the proof and we get it into the right hands."

"But—"

"You're not in this alone anymore. We'll figure it out together, okay?"

He thought she might argue, but she nodded. "Together."

He slipped his arm back around her shoulder and they began walking again. They needed to get as far from here as possible.

THEY USED THE last of the cash to take a taxi across town. Luke needed to talk to his brothers and couldn't take a chance on anything being bugged.

Claire donned the brown wig, and they walked a couple of miles before calling a cab at a hotel. If Ballard was smart, he would have the media put a picture of Khan all over the TV. He was much more noticeable than either Luke or Claire was. People would be recording them left and right if they needed to look for the giant cat.

Luke and Claire talked as little as possible in the cab. He didn't want the driver to have any reason to remember them. He had the driver take them to a small mall a couple of miles away from the San Antonio Security office. He hated to make her walk more, but it was better this way.

He knew she was surprised when he led her into an underground parking garage a couple of blocks from his office. They took the elevator back up to the ground-level floor, then walked down the hallway and out the back door.

It led out to the alley that led between the two buildings. It gave him and the guys a second hidden entrance into their office. It was one of the primary reasons they chose this particular space to rent.

If someone were watching their building, they would still never know Luke and Claire were inside.

The relief on his brothers' faces was apparent as soon as they came in through the back door.

"Thank God," Brax murmured.

Weston and Chance immediately closed the blinds on the front window. The glass was tinted, but this gave them an extra measure of privacy.

Brax sat down and switched on the signal blocker. That would block anyone attempting to use audio surveillance equipment to listen in on their conversations.

"Are you guys all right?" Brax asked. "When we heard about the Wars Hill library fire, we immediately got over there but we couldn't find any sign of you."

Luke led Claire so she could sit on the small couch in the corner of the waiting room. Khan immediately jumped up into her lap.

He gave Weston a look, who immediately nodded, knowing what they needed. Weston headed toward the small kitchen and dug up something for them to eat and drink.

"We hid, then sneaked out a bathroom window. I got quite a few stitches for my trouble."

Claire winced and he reached over and grabbed her hand, rubbing his thumb across her knuckles.

"If you thought everyone was looking for you before, it's definitely worse now that they think you shot a cop."

Both Luke and Brax shot Chance a look when Claire let out a shuddered breath. Chance didn't mean any harm by his words; he just didn't pull any punches. Luke was gruff in the same way, and actually prided himself on it.

But not when it came to Claire. He didn't want anyone to do or say anything to upset her. She'd been through enough.

"Sorry," Chance muttered.

"No, you're right," Claire whispered. "Did he die?"

Brax shook his head. "Weston put in a call to see what he could find out. It's still touch-and-go, but there's a chance he'll pull through."

"Any chance he would be able to identify who shot him if he makes it?" Luke asked. It wouldn't solve all their problems, but at least they wouldn't be after Claire as a cop killer.

Chance shook his head. "It seems unlikely given the trajectory of the bullet that hit him, and we only know that because of what Weston was able to get from his cop friends."

"My vote is for you to turn yourself in." Weston walked back in the room and handed a plate of sandwiches and a couple of water bottles to Luke, who nodded his thanks. "There are good cops in the San Antonio PD. You two can back up each other's statements. Otherwise, they are going to be after you in full force after what happened at the library."

"That's what I wanted to do." Claire sat up straighter on the couch. "Luke has already gotten hurt—"

All three of his brothers stiffened.

"How bad?"

"Do we need a doctor?"

"Status."

It was impossible to tell who was saying what with them talking all over one another.

"I'm fine. Nothing that couldn't be fixed by breaking in at a local vet's clinic. It wasn't a big deal."

"And if I hadn't been there to hit that guy in the head with the skateboard? He would've shot you."

Luke picked up half of a sandwich from the plate on his lap and stuck it in Claire's mouth.

"Yes, Ballard and his men are dangerous. Deadly, even. And that's why you can't go to the cops." He turned to his brothers. "Ballard would've already thought of that. He has to have a plan in place if she goes running to the cops and claims her innocence."

"I should've done that from the beginning. I should've walked out of Passage Digital and gone straight to the police. I don't trust cops. I don't like people. I'm so stupid." Luke took the sandwich back out of her hands.

"Hey." He cupped her cheeks with his hands. "Maybe… Maybe you might've been able to catch Ballard before he could get any stopgap measures in place, but probably not. He's too wealthy and too well-connected to not have been able to handle that.

The most likely thing that would've happened is that you'd be dead right now and my whole world would be crushed without me even knowing it."

"I just don't want you to get hurt. I don't want anyone else to get hurt."

Luke could never have been much of a poet. No one had ever accused him of being in touch with his sensitive side. But suddenly, he had a very clear understanding of what drowning in someone's eyes meant. He couldn't have escaped the hypnotic pull of Claire's baby blues even if he had wanted to.

And he very definitely didn't want to. What he definitely did want to do was kiss her, but he couldn't with his brothers staring at them.

"So, we need a plan that involves Claire not going to the police," Brax said. "Anybody got one of those?"

"Not yet." Luke forced himself to look away from Claire. "We're going to go to ground until we figure out a way to get the proof we need."

Weston leaned back against the wall and crossed his arms over his chest. "That works as a temporary measure, but unless you plan to be on the run for the rest of your lives, it can't be permanent. They'll be after you, too, soon, Luke. Right now, there's no ties between the two of you but once there is, you could be arrested for aiding and abetting."

"That could affect…things," Brax said, his usual charming smile nowhere to be found.

Luke nodded. He knew exactly what his brother meant.

"What things?" Claire asked, feeding a piece of chicken to Khan. "Bad things?"

Luke didn't want to tell her.

"In this together, remember?" she whispered.

He scrubbed a hand over his face. "If I'm charged with aiding and abetting, or any crime really, it could affect a lot of things with our business. The licenses we're able to hold, our relationship with law enforcement…"

"Oh."

He wanted to tell her it was worth it to him, all of it…even if it meant losing everything. But it wasn't just him this affected. San Antonio Security was part of all of them. And he loved his brothers.

"I think you do need to go to ground. Get out of Dodge," Chance said.

Luke turned to him. "What about the business?"

"Go to the cops first. Clear your name and distance yourself from this."

Luke could almost see Chance's strategic mind working.

"Tell the cops the truth, but the selective truth. Tell them that Claire came to you, a pretty lady all big eyes and sad story. You two knew each other as kids. She was broke, but you put her up at a hotel and were supposed to meet the next morning but evidently, she took off in the middle of the night. Next thing you knew, her photo was all over the news."

Luke caught Claire's flinch out of the corner of his eye. He grabbed her hand. "None of that is true."

"All of it is true," she scoffed.

"Hey." Brax smiled at her. "Those statement may be true but they're not all the facts. We know all the facts, and that's what matters.

Claire didn't look very relieved.

They all turned to Weston. "Would this work?" Luke asked. "You have the most experience with law enforcement."

"Maybe. Probably. You keep it as general as possible, giving the cops what they already know. We have a good reputation—you have a good reputation—so there's no reason for them not to believe you."

"We'll get your truck out of the vicinity of the library so nothing is traced back to you," Brax said.

"Is it possible that they'll arrest me? Maybe I shouldn't go at all."

Because he damn well wouldn't be able to protect her behind bars. She'd be on her own.

"Think about your life, Luke. This company. You can't ruin your reputation."

"San Antonio Security is not more important than your life, Claire. I don't want to leave you alone unprotected."

"We'll keep her safe if something happens to you," Brax said, and both Weston and Chance were beside him, nodding their agreement. "You'll probably only be with the police for a few hours, tops. But however long it is, we've got your back."

"Both of your backs," Weston said.

Chapter Fifteen

Luke glanced to his right in time for amber light to wash over Claire's face. She was sleeping, which brought him a small measure of peace after a long day.

Weighing everything now as he headed out of town on the last leg of their journey, he knew he should be glad they'd made it out. And he was. But it hadn't been anything he'd want to do again.

Like the seven hours he'd spent with Detectives Arellano and Fisher.

He had a hard time believing neither of them was dirty, or at least being pushed from behind by the large, firm hand of one Vance Ballard. Weston still couldn't offer insight into the two of them, which meant he had no way of smoothing things over or asking them to pull back a little. They weren't his former colleagues, unlike the local San Antonio cops.

Luke had known that going in.

But seven hours of constant questions had worn his nerves to their breaking point. No amount of preparation could keep his frustration at bay, though he'd fought against it until the end. He repeated the story

he and his brothers had come up with, right down to
the smallest detail, giving neither detective so much
as an inch they could slide a wedge into.

If he'd been frustrated, they'd been near the end of
their ropes by the time the questioning wrapped up.
It was clear they had an end in mind, a goal—drawing connections between him and Claire, figuring out
what role he played in this. Whether they could use
him to get to her or not.

They'd had no idea who they were dealing with
going into the questioning. He figured they had a
pretty good idea by the time they'd finished, though.

"Do you really want to protect a murderer?" Fisher
had asked more than once.

"You know she shot that cop, too, right?" Arellano
had demanded. Luke still wondered, hours later, how
much the two of them knew. Whether they believed
Claire had been behind it or if they were aware of
Ballard's henchmen.

Better to stick to the prepared answers Weston had
helped coach him through before the interrogation.
Claire was appealing, big-eyed and in need of protection. He hadn't asked too many questions because he
couldn't have imagined she'd be wrapped up in something this big. She'd asked for help, had made him feel
like the only one who could provide it—she'd played
on his protective instincts.

Even as the words had soured in his mouth, he'd
watched understanding dawn on the faces of the men
in front of him. Probably identifying with the senti-

ment. He was surprised his teeth were still intact after grinding them so hard.

In the end, there'd been no way to prove he wasn't telling the full truth, and no way to connect him and Claire. Even if they knew about her time in the Skyline Park group home, his name hadn't been Patterson then.

His release had come as a relief, but not a total win because they'd still be watching.

Which meant doing something he couldn't have imagined being capable of at this particular time—going into the office like it was an ordinary day and pretending to work for hours. All that had kept him in place was knowing Claire was safe. Brax had taken her someplace and was guarding her while Luke and the rest kept up the charade of everything being status quo.

One memory of those long, tense hours made him smile—the fact that two weeks' worth of filing had been done for him by Maci Ford, the new office manager his brothers had hired. His office was much easier to kill time in without those files staring at him. It would be nice to meet the person responsible for that.

Once this was over. Once life felt like life again.

For the afternoon, all he could do was look forward to being with Claire. He trusted Brax with his life, but there was nothing that could touch the certainty of having her in his arms. Seeing as how Brax couldn't tell him where he'd planned to take Claire for the sake of keeping Luke honest when he claimed he had no idea where she was, his anxiety had been through the roof.

Even Luke was impressed with what his brother had come up with. Chance always was the tactical mastermind. He'd found four cars of the same make and model, and working together, they'd crisscrossed all over town. Trading cars in parking lots, beneath overpasses. Talking on the phone all the while, just in case anyone was listening, comparing notes on their favorite teams and player stats the way any group of brothers would. Like there was nothing out of the ordinary going on.

That was what outsiders didn't understand, and it was the Pattersons' most powerful weapon—the fact that they were brothers, not simply business associates. They'd go out of their way to have one another's backs, would spend hours leading anyone on their trail on a wild-goose chase. All for the sake of protecting one of them.

And what mattered most in the world to him.

After two hours, Luke had finally landed in the car holding Claire and Khan in the back seat, the two of them lying low to avoid notice. That was when he'd finally been able to breathe without a weight on his chest. Chance had continued the game with the tail following his car, thinking Luke was the driver.

Luke, meanwhile, was on his way out of town with his woman and her cat-dog safe and secure.

He was only a few miles away from his destination. Nobody knew about this place. It wasn't even on the grid, using a generator and solar panels to keep it powered up. The perfect hiding spot.

Though that wasn't what his parents had intended, obviously. Back in the day, it was a getaway. Somewhere to disconnect from the pressures of the world, somewhere for their dad to teach them to fish, where they could breathe fresh air outside the city.

In other words, an ideal location for him and Claire to spend a few days. She needed the rest, needed to feel secure for a little while. They could come up with a plan for moving forward once they had the time to reset.

He was still thinking along those lines as he turned off the main road onto the rocky trail leading up to the cabin. The change in terrain left the car swaying a little, which stirred Claire into wakefulness. "Is this Lake Conroe?" she mumbled, still sleepy.

Even now, she struck him as hopelessly adorable, rubbing sleep from her eyes before immediately looking to check on Khan. "Almost. Just a few minutes more."

"I can't wait to stretch my legs."

"I'll bet. Cramped up in a car for hours." But she'd held on, going with the flow. She might've been the strongest woman he knew, except for maybe his mom.

That thought lingered in his mind as he pulled closer to the cabin.

And found the lights on inside.

"Oh," Claire breathed. "For some reason, I thought the cabin would be empty."

"It should be…" He brought them to a stop, staring at the familiar structure with his mouth open.

She went stiff. "Are we in trouble?"

It was almost laughable. And he would've laughed if this latest twist didn't complicate things even further. "No, we're not in trouble. It's just that this is happening earlier than I thought it would." He got out of the car, shaking his head.

"What's that mean?" Claire followed him, a note of fear in her voice even after he'd told her it was okay. She'd pulled Khan out of the car with her and held him to her chest, protective and a little scared.

"It means you're about to meet my parents." He put an arm around her waist and pulled her toward the house before she could ask any more questions or, even more likely, plant her feet and refuse to take another step.

Timing had never been his parents' strong suit, but how were they supposed to know?

"Well, what's this?" Clinton bolted up from his chair at the opening of the door, and a huge smile threatened to crack his face wide open. "What a great surprise!"

Sheila came in from the kitchen, wiping her hands on her apron. "Luke! How terrific! I was just thinking about you!"

He'd only just been thinking about her, but there wasn't time to explain that without explaining a great deal more about Claire than he was comfortable with just then. Besides, there were more important things to talk about.

Such as, who Claire was, for starters.

"Claire, these are my parents, Clinton and Sheila Patterson." Not the way he'd hoped to introduce her one day, but these were strange times. "Mom and Dad, this is Claire."

He didn't know what else to say. Certainly, he couldn't go into detail. He didn't even want to use her last name since they might've heard it on the news.

The two of them jumped into action, with Clinton directing Claire to the chair he'd just vacated. "You two look half-starved," Sheila decided. "I was just putting supper on. And look at that gorgeous cat! I'm sure I can dig up a little something for you, too."

Either Khan understood English or his instincts were sharp enough to know who he needed to become best friends with. He took his leave from Claire and trotted into the kitchen on Sheila's heels. Clinton added wood to the fire. "The cabin's been closed up for a while now, and you'll find the nights get fairly cool this time of year."

Neither of them asked questions, either because they knew better than to delve into their sons' lives—no telling where their work led them or how much they could share—or because they had enough tact not to make things awkward.

That was one thing the two of them had to spare, tact. It was what had made them ideal foster parents to four wounded, scared boys. They knew when to ask questions and when to leave well enough alone.

Before he knew it, the four of them were seated around the kitchen table, and Sheila was piling pasta on Claire's plate. "One thing you learn as a mother to four boys is how to quickly double a meal. I swear, I don't know how I managed to keep the kitchen stocked in those days." She added vegetables to the plate before handing it over. Ever a parent.

"It must've been…interesting." Claire's gaze darted over to Luke, a tiny smile tugging at the corners of her mouth.

"Oh, sweetheart, it was a real challenge sometimes. Well, it was!" Sheila laughed when Luke rolled his eyes. "The four of you were so spirited and stubborn. Remember the one trip we took up here, where you almost drowned yourself in the lake? Convinced you'd caught a big one."

"It was a tire." Clinton laughed. "And I warned him, I did, but he insisted he'd caught something legendary. Lost his balance and ended up in water over his head."

"This was before he learned to swim, mind you." Sheila shook her head, laughing. "Life wasn't boring, I'll tell you that much."

Luke couldn't help but marvel at his mother's ability to draw Claire out of her shell. They weren't more than a few minutes into the meal before she was laughing, not to mention the way she tore into her supper like she hadn't eaten in ages. It did him good to see her with an appetite.

It was just like being a kid again, when he'd first arrived at the Patterson home. How scared and wounded and untrusting he'd been. How Sheila had worked her way into his trust, how she hadn't pushed but instead pulled him into the warmth of her love with food and laughter, letting him come around in his own good time.

He could almost forget what was happening around them, the cloud hanging over their heads. It all felt so right, being there with her, sitting down with his parents…like Claire was already part of the family.

There was no more awkwardness until it came time to turn in. Naturally, his parents expected to take the master bedroom with its king-size bed.

Leaving the second bedroom to Luke and Claire.

"Bunk beds." Claire's amusement was evident, no matter how she tried to hide it.

"Two sets." He leaned against one set with a sigh as memories bumped against each other, almost too many for him to handle.

"This is where you boys slept?"

"Mm-hmm."

"Which bed was yours?"

He jerked a thumb toward the top bunk just behind him and Claire nodded. "I want that one."

"You're serious?"

"I am. What?" she asked when he chuckled. "I want to sleep in the bed you slept in. Is that funny?"

Funny? No. In fact, it was sort of sexy in a weird way. He kept that thought to himself in favor of sliding his arms around her waist. "Not much room for more than one person in these beds."

"Good thing I'm too wiped out to think about anything but sleep right now." But she was smiling, and for a moment, it was almost possible to forget there was anything more important happening in their lives than an unforeseen meeting with his parents.

"I'm glad you got to meet them, even if this wasn't what I had planned." He pressed a kiss against her forehead while her arms linked around his neck.

"They're wonderful people."

"They are. I had no doubt you'd get along with them."

"And they love you. That much is obvious." She stood on her tiptoes to kiss him softly, almost playfully. "I mean, not that I blame them or anything. You're pretty wonderful, too."

"Mom's superpower is loving," he murmured, careful to keep his voice low, the way they used to when they were kids pretending to be asleep. "They're perfect for each other, those two. They are both very special people."

Claire changed into pajamas and climbed into her bunk while Khan took the bottom bunk across from her. Watchful, but comfortable in his own right. "Keep an eye on her," Luke whispered to the cat once Claire was sound asleep.

THE CABIN WAS DARK, quiet, though Luke knew better than to accept things at face value. His father would want to talk. They'd only exchanged a single long look before retiring to their respective bedrooms, but that look had carried a lot of weight.

He was waiting on the small porch overlooking the lake. The water was still and smooth under a cloudless sky, giving the illusion of there being two moons thanks to a motionless reflection. "Beautiful," Luke whispered. There was nothing like being out here, away from the rest of the world.

Clinton nodded, staring off in the same direction. "I recognize your friend from TV."

"It's not what you think."

"I figured as much."

"We only need to lie low for a few days. It'll give us time to regroup and come up with a plan. The people after her are dangerous and connected enough to use law enforcement as a personal tool to catch her."

"Your brothers are helping?"

"As much as they can."

"Who is this girl that she's important enough for you to go to all this trouble?"

"I knew her back at Skyline Park. She was important to me then. She still is."

Clinton sighed, finally turning his face toward his son. "You know your mom won't want to leave now, not with another baby bird to take care of. But I can't put her in a situation where she might be in danger, either. Not with her blood pressure."

"I wouldn't want to put her in danger, believe me."

"That being said, if you think it's okay, we'll stay tomorrow. Give her a chance to mother you both for a while. It'll do her good."

"I think it'll do Claire good, too." He didn't bother mentioning himself, as his needs were fairly far down on the priority list. But he suspected it would do him good, just the same.

They fell into an easy silence while nature's sounds

filled the air. Even at night, there was never real, true quiet. An owl's cry pierced the air. Leaves rustled. There were sounds of scurrying as some small animal foraged for its supper.

At least they had a natural alarm system all around them. If intruders decided to approach, the animals would sound an alert.

Luke's heart swelled when he looked over at his dad, whose profile stood out against the moonlit sky. They didn't share blood, but Clinton had taught him everything he knew about being a man and about what mattered in life. He'd set Luke's feet on the path they currently trod.

"I know that whatever you do, it'll be the right thing," Clinton decided. "I don't know a lot of things, but that much I know for sure."

Luke hoped his father was right.

Chapter Sixteen

Claire woke the next morning and found herself trapped in a family sitcom out of the 1950s.

The mom wore an apron and bustled around the kitchen, laughing and rolling her eyes at her husband's terrible jokes. Their pride in their son shone through every time he was in the room, as did the love and respect they had for each other.

Definitely something out of a '50s sitcom, except the dad was Black, the mom was Puerto Rican, their son was white, and their guest was a wanted fugitive.

It was all a little surreal, especially when she had never fit in at her foster homes. Most of them hadn't been bad; nobody had been mean to her, except for the people at Skyline Park.

Even so, she'd been the quiet kid. The one who wasn't good with people, who slipped through the cracks. Foster families tended to be full and busy, the parents already stretched thin by trying to provide for all the kids in their care.

None of them had set out to ignore her. It had been easy to do since she was the kid who basically wanted nothing more than to be left alone. The squeaky wheel got the oil, the quiet wheel ended up alone with a cat.

That wasn't the case with Sheila Patterson. Nobody was left out when she was around.

She'd coddled Luke ever since finding out about his wound, looking after it, making him his favorite foods.

More surprising? Luke had let her do it.

He loved her and she loved him. Nothing could be more evident. And the more evident it became, the more Claire found herself withdrawing. Not on purpose. It was what she did whenever she was on the outside looking in.

But Sheila was having none of it.

She'd included Claire in every conversation. Every game of spades. Cooking, washing dishes—Sheila included her in that, too. She didn't treat Claire like a guest; she treated her like family.

It was amazing and alarming, like nothing Claire had ever known. Yet every time she started to withdraw and shut down, some member of the Patterson family pulled her back in.

"Mom." Luke found Claire and Sheila in the kitchen, and he didn't look happy. "Dad is dragging me down to the lake so he can show me his new rod and reel. Please tell me you have something I can do here so I don't have to go. Like scrubbing toilets."

He sounded like a whiny little kid and Claire couldn't help but smile.

Sheila sighed with a shrug. "I'm afraid you're going to have to go fishing with your father. I'm going to teach Claire how to make apple turnovers."

That was news to Claire, though the fact that the mere mention of turnovers made Luke's eyes literally light up told her this was a good way to spend the time. "You are?"

"That way she has something to lord over you when you're not behaving the way you should." Sheila dropped a knowing wink Claire's way.

Luke shook his head. "You're a cruel woman, Sheila Patterson. Equipping the younger generation to operate in that way."

Sheila raised one dark eyebrow. "We women have to stick together."

Luke was still grumbling good-naturedly as he and Clinton walked down to the creek that fed into the lake. Meanwhile, Claire had the feeling this situation was a setup to give Sheila a chance for them to talk privately.

She tried to keep a positive expression on her face, but she couldn't help but worry. Sheila might not have been related to Luke by blood, but she thought of herself as his mother.

And undoubtedly, thought of Claire as a threat to her son.

The irony of the situation didn't escape her as Sheila took her through the process, step-by-step. There was nothing Claire wanted more than to know how to make Luke's favorite dessert, though ideally, she'd make it when he wasn't in danger because of her. She was only learning the recipe because they'd come here to hide out for a while.

There was also a sense of waiting for the other

shoe to drop—for Sheila's tone to change as she took Claire through the steps. When was she going to get around to it?

As it turned out, Sheila got around to it while Claire was busy folding the homemade pastry dough around apple slices. "Luke is important to me. All of my sons are." She didn't stop working as she spoke, so Claire didn't, either.

"I could see that. He loves you and Clinton, and you both love him. I'm so happy he found a family who appreciates him."

Sheila glanced over at her. "And you? Do you appreciate Luke the way he is?"

"Luke was my hero when we were kids. He looked after me when we were in the group home together. I guess he's still my hero."

Sheila smiled a mother's knowing smile. "He's always been very protective. It's his nature. It's easy to see he's protective toward you, even more than normal. He cares about you."

"I care about him, too," Claire whispered.

"He doesn't talk much about his life before us. We know about Skyline Park, of course, and what a terrible place it was before it got shut down. I'm sorry you were there. I hope it wasn't too bad."

"It would've been much worse if it hadn't been for Luke." She forced herself to look Sheila in the eye in spite of her nervousness and the sense of being judged by a protective mother. "I don't want to complicate his life. I want him to be safe and happy. I don't know how much you know about how we ended up in each other's lives again, but the last thing I want is to complicate things for him."

"I believe you." Sheila pointed to the turnover Claire was working on. "Make sure that seal is tight or the juice will run out."

And that was that. Sheila seemed satisfied, and Claire had the sense of having passed a test—maybe the most critical test she'd ever taken.

BY EVENING, it was just the two of them. Clinton and Sheila had gone home, but not before Sheila made sure they had plenty of food for a few days and a clean cabin to stay in. "Take care of each other," she'd whispered in Claire's ear as they hugged goodbye.

Luke certainly looked and sounded like he was well taken care of as he finished his third turnover. "She taught you well," he groaned, patting his belly. "Too well. I might end up popping the button off my pants after this dessert."

"Your parents are amazing. It's easy to see how you boys turned out so well. You got so lucky."

"We did." He took her hand and slid his thumb over the knuckles. "I wish you had, too. I want you to know that. I've been wondering ever since we got here and found my parents if you were thinking about how our lives diverged."

"If you're asking whether I'm jealous or not, the answer is no." She meant it with all her heart. She would have never held Luke's good luck against him. "I want the best for you. That's what it's all about, right? And you got the best, no doubt."

He pulled her in for a kiss. "I sure did."

If her first full day at the cabin had been something out of a sitcom, the next two days were a happy
dream—an idyllic, perfect little dream full of nature's beauty and peace. The joy of being together,
of making love all through the night and sleeping in
each other's arms.

There was fun, too. Like when Luke took her fishing, knowing she didn't have the first clue about it.
"Wait. You mean I have to stick the hook through the
worm?"

"How did you think this went? I'm genuinely curious."

"I thought I went to the store and whoops, there
was fish in the case. Can we not, I don't know…drag
a net through the water and see what we pick up?"

"I mean, we could," he offered as he hooked a
worm, "but that would take a lot of time. And, you
know, a boat. We can fish from the banks. But hey, at
least we'll have the fun of cleaning the fish we catch.
Aren't you looking forward to that?"

Only the fact that she caught twice as many trout
as he did made the day salvageable. That, and the
company—the stories he told and the way his entire
demeanor changed as he relaxed. She had no doubt he
was still on guard, that his skilled gaze took in everything around them and processed it for signs of trouble, but he did his best to be in the moment with her.

She couldn't have loved him more if she tried.

This might be their life one day. She reflected on
that while they sat together on the porch, side by side

in rocking chairs. There was peace and quiet, the sort of quiet that settled on a person's heart and spread all through them, making everything a little sweeter. A little better.

And he might be hers. For always. If he wanted to be.

She had the feeling he did, and it made her heart swell with pride and hope. If they could only think about that right now…if only there wasn't so much in the way.

"What are you thinking about?" He turned to her with a smile, amber light all around his head cast from the setting sun. He looked like the angel he'd always been to her.

"How sweet this is. How I needed this." She let out a long sigh, gazing out over the lake. "How I would love to come back here someday…when I'm not afraid anymore."

His hand closed over hers, giving her strength. "You don't have to be afraid."

"Luke…"

"I know it's easy for me to say, but I'm in this for the long haul. Whatever it takes. You have me, and you have my brothers. You have Sheila and Clinton Patterson at your back. In case you couldn't tell, they're a force to be reckoned with."

"You don't need to tell me that." She laughed. "Anybody who could keep you boys in order has my full confidence."

"They like you. I could tell."

"That is a massive compliment." She winked with

a smile. "I liked them, too. A lot. They didn't have to be so nice to me, so welcoming. Here I am, a random person they'd never met before, walking into their special cabin."

"Love is what they do. It's who they are."

"I see a lot of them in you." He snickered a little and she continued, "No, I do. You're the same person you always were, don't get me wrong—you're still kind and brave. But you're not as afraid to show it now as you used to be when we were kids."

"You bring it out in me, too, Kitten. It's not all my parents. It's you." He stood, pulling her to her feet and wrapping her in one of his all-encompassing hugs. "It's always been you."

She hadn't made a ton of good decisions in her life, and she knew it.

And while she regretted dragging Luke into the insanity, she couldn't help but think that walking into his office was one of the best decisions she'd ever made.

"I wish we could stay here forever," she admitted in a soft, shaky whisper, wrapped up tight in his arms.

"Me too, Kitten," he whispered, stroking her hair. "Me, too."

Chapter Seventeen

"Let me get this straight."

Vance Ballard leaned forward, his hands folded atop his desk. Could the pair of useless idiots standing before him see how tightly he'd clenched his fingers? His joints ached, yet the discomfort kept him sharp, focused.

And as long as his hands were folded, he couldn't reach for the paperweight sitting on one corner of the desk and throw it at them.

Brooks and Masters did what they could to conceal their growing discomfort. He gave them at least a bit of credit for delivering yet more bad news to his face. Surely even a pair of idiots had to know how their update would be received.

He spoke slowly, with care. "A nothing. A nobody with no family, no friends and hardly any past has managed to elude you. *Again*."

Brooks cleared his throat. "Sir, there's nothing any of us can come up with to explain it. We're missing something."

"So are those detectives," Masters blurted it out,

bringing to mind a child tattling on their sibling. "They've been following those Patterson guys around; they questioned the one she went to but they didn't find anything to connect her to them."

More discomfort, this time resulting from Ballard gritting his teeth to hold back a string of bitter profanity. "And we're certain she doesn't have a bank account or credit card we haven't discovered?"

"If she had anything, we would know. No one can get past our monitoring," Brooks insisted in a far steadier voice than that of his partner.

Ballard knew this was true, though the truth of it only infuriated him further. She couldn't access her money. She had nowhere to run. Yet she'd run and continued to elude capture.

How was she doing it? He could've turned the office upside down, but that wouldn't have brought Claire Wallace to him. How could she get past him? *No one got past him.*

"The library fire... We know she had help." He looked at his men, who were increasingly useless. "She couldn't have pulled that off on her own. And Hopkins was clear on there being a man with her." There had been thick smoke at the time, and Hopkins had sustained a head injury moments after seeing the man, but no amount of questioning could shake his certainty.

Claire had the help of a man that night.

"Hopkins didn't see the man," Masters mumbled. "Or, rather, he doesn't remember what he looked like.

The smoke was too thick and his memory's hazy. But there was—"

"I know. There was definitely a man. Don't tell me what I already know." A lot of good it did them, knowing about the presence of someone who surely had to exist. No way would Claire be able to manage that escape on her own. The presence of another person came as no surprise.

There was a ticking noise in the back of his mind, the sound of precious seconds slipping away. Was she enjoying this? That useless, pathetic—

After slowly releasing a deep breath, Ballard asked, "And reports from the detectives confirm she wasn't with that Patterson man after they questioned him?"

"He went to the office, stayed there all day, ran a couple of errands." Masters looked to Brooks, who offered a slight nod in agreement.

"They missed something…they must have. The police are not looking in the right places." Ballard clenched his fists beneath the desk, out of sight. He barely flinched when discomfort slid into pain. It kept him focused. Kept displeasure from turning into fury.

"We'll keep looking," Brooks offered, though there was uncertainty in his voice. He doubted the usefulness of this course of action because he wasn't a complete moron.

"No, there are other ways. More efficient ways. Perhaps a bit messier, but in the end, they'll serve our purpose more effectively than searching for a needle in a haystack. I want that girl's world to dwindle to the size of a pinprick. I want her terrified. I want her to scurry for cover, because that's when she'll make a mistake that will allow us to ensnare her. When she's most unsettled."

"And then?"

For the first time in days, Ballard smiled. "And then we'll kill her."

"GIVE ME THE RUNDOWN."

Claire paused in the middle of drying the last of the dinner dishes. She'd known Luke was on the phone with his brothers—the only people who'd know how to get in contact with him on his burner phone.

It was the tone in his voice that stopped her and made her listen. She held her breath, though that didn't do much to quiet the pounding in her ears.

Luke muttered a curse that made her flinch. "You're sure about that? What's their status?" Another curse, delivered with the sort of bitterness that nearly curdled her blood.

She was still holding a plate. Best to put it down before she dropped it. There was no way Luke was about to deliver good news, and for some reason, in the middle of the fluttery panic threatening to take control of her mind, she felt it extremely important to take care of Sheila and Clinton's things. They had been good to her, and she didn't want them to regret even a broken plate.

He was in the living room, standing with his back to her as she tiptoed out of the kitchen. He might as well have been made of stone—so still, so tense. He'd been still for so long that it almost came as a surprise when he ended the call and slid the phone into his pocket.

"What is it?" she choked out. "What's happened? And don't tell me it's nothing because I know something bad's going on."

"I wasn't going to tell you it's nothing." He turned his head, giving her a look at his profile. "I was trying to figure out how to tell you, is all."

"Maybe you should come out with it and get it over with. I can handle it."

He let out a deep breath as his shoulders fell. "There've been problems. That was Weston on the phone, giving me reports from the police department. A truck was run off the road into a ravine overnight. The driver didn't make it."

He might as well have broken out in Greek for all the sense he was making. "If the driver didn't make it, then how do the police know they were run off the road?"

"There were skid marks on the road, along with damage to the rear of the truck. Like another vehicle pushed it." A ghost of a smile played over his lips. "You would think to ask that, even now."

"I still don't understand what this has to do with anything."

"We might not have made a connection if it wasn't for the fire."

She was more lost than ever. "Fire?"

He crossed the small room in three strides and took her by the arms. "I'm sorry, but the Romero house went up last night… It burned to the ground. There were at least two people inside when it did. The bodies haven't been identified yet, but it seems likely your foster parents were home. When Weston got word, something clicked. He checked on the identity of the truck's driver… It was Glen Parker. I'm so sorry."

"Another foster parent." They'd killed her foster parents, people she hadn't seen in ages. The Romeros had always kept her in mind, even after she'd left them. The Parkers had always been kind.

The world started to gray at the edges. Luke's voice started to fade.

"Claire. Stay with me." His hands tightened, squeezing her biceps a little.

It had the intended effect. The world sharpened again, no matter how she wished it wouldn't.

People were dead because of her, good people. She'd been only one of many kids taken in by them. Life might not have been perfect or even fun all the time, but it had been better than living on the street and eating out of trash cans. They had spared so many kids so much danger and pain.

And now? The thought of them dying in terror and pain threatened to crush her. If it wasn't for Luke, she might've crumpled to the floor and never gotten up.

"You didn't do this." He took her in his arms and held her close. "This isn't your fault. You need to know that."

"In my head, I know it." She closed her eyes as she buried her face in his chest.

"But it's another story once we reach your heart. Right?"

"Right."

"I understand. I do." He stroked her hair, soothing her at least a little. "You couldn't know what he would do. Only a truly sick, twisted person could dream up something like this. A means of smoking you out."

"I can't have him hurt anybody else. I can't let that happen." She pulled back enough to look up into his eyes. There were as many questions there as she had running through her head…doubts, too. Was he wondering if they'd make it out of this the way she did?

One thing she knew—even if he did have doubts, he would never voice those doubts in front of her. He would try to be strong the way he always did.

She could be strong, too.

"I'll turn myself in. Listen," she insisted when he grimaced, "it's the only way. I should've done it in the first place. I could've gotten ahead of this somehow, ahead of him. I was too busy trying to be clever."

"You did the only thing you could do given the circumstances."

"And look where it got me. Look where it got them. This is the only way to stop the bleeding, you know what I mean? Put an end to it, go in and tell the police everything."

"I need you to listen to me." He leaned in until his face was the only thing in her field of vision. There were no more questions or doubts in his eyes. "You go in and there's no protection for you. Those detectives—the ones who questioned me—can't be the only ones under his influence. There are more, so many more, and one or more of them will get to you. They'll find a split second when you're outside the range of a security camera and that'll be that. He will have you killed. Do you understand?"

Funny how speaking became impossible with the threat of her murder dangling in front of her. She could only nod.

"I don't want to scare you, but that's just the way it is." His eyes darted over her face. "Do you understand?"

"I do." She struggled to say the words.

"The only way to get through this is to work together. We have to come up with a plan. We've outsmarted him so far. We just have to keep outsmarting him until he's beat. Do you believe we can do this together?"

There were moments in Claire's life when she'd known nothing but doubt, but this wasn't one of those moments. "I believe you."

"Good." His eyes shone. "That's as good a place to start as any, I guess."

Chapter Eighteen

Trying to sleep was a waste of time.

What was not a waste, however, was lying in bed with Claire in his arms.

She was asleep, her breathing soft and even. She whimpered every once in a while but would relax when his arms tightened. Like she knew she could trust him even when sleeping.

Now he had to earn that trust.

Which was probably why he couldn't sleep to save his life.

So many factors, so many possibilities. A man like Ballard had a lot of connections, a lot of ties. Like a weed-strewn lawn. Pulling up everything they saw would only get them so far, since weeds spread underground, too. Tomorrow morning there'd be more, and more after that.

How to put an end to it once and for all?

He had to be smarter. Think clearer.

How was he supposed to think clearly when the only woman in the world who'd ever mattered was asleep in his arms, trusting him, needing him? It had never been as important as it was just then to rise above it all, look down at it, see it. Plan a way out.

It had never been more impossible.

She stirred and he went still, careful not to wake her. At least one of them should be well-rested.

But it was no use. She lifted her head from his chest, blinking away sleep. "Mmm?"

"Mmm?" Even now, he couldn't help but grin at how cute she was.

"Did you say something?" Her voice was thick but still sweet.

"No. You might've been dreaming. Go back to sleep."

"Not if you're awake."

"I'll go to sleep, too," he offered.

She touched his cheek with tender fingertips. "Something tells me you haven't been asleep at all."

"You're sharp, Kitten." He bent one arm, propping his head up on his forearm with a groan. "I've been too busy thinking to sleep. But one of us should, if we can."

"I kept having bad dreams, anyway," she admitted. "It's easier to be awake, when my subconscious doesn't make things seem so real."

"I'm sorry." He stroked her silky hair, letting it run between his fingers like a golden waterfall. When this was over, he would take a solid day and devote it to nothing but this—the simple pleasure of touching her.

"What are we going to do?" He knew it wasn't a question she expected him to answer, at least not right away.

"We've spent all this time on the defensive, right? Running away, hiding, barely escaping. He hasn't backed down an inch—if anything, it's made him more determined than ever. He's getting desperate. Going after the people who were once a part of your life, at least the ones he can trace. He figures he has to cut out anybody who could be helping you until you have nowhere left to turn."

"Until I figure the only way out is to turn myself in," she whispered, cringing. "Which is exactly the impulse I almost followed."

"It's not your fault. He knows you're a decent person with a soul and a conscience. He might not have either for himself, but he knows they exist in other people. He wanted to prey on that. We're still smarter than he is. We won't fall into his trap."

"So what will we do?"

"We'll go on the attack. We'll turn the tables on him."

"How? He'll know in a heartbeat if I try to hack him again. He'll be waiting for that."

"I know. I'm not talking about hacking."

"What are you talking about?" She pushed herself up on one arm and looked down at him. "What are you thinking?"

"I'm thinking we use his weaknesses against him."

"How do you know he has any?"

"Everybody has a weakness, Kitten. One of the things I've had to learn in my business was how to figure out what those weaknesses are. They're a way inside." His breath caught when he realized what he was saying.

She knew it, too. "The way Ballard's been using my weaknesses to flush me out."

"I'm sorry."

Chewing on her lip, she lifted a shoulder. "Okay. So, we'll use my skills to find his weaknesses. You know by now that I can hack my way into anything. There's got to be information about him some-where—though knowing him, he's done everything he can to hide it so nobody can find it."

"We don't have to find his personal weaknesses, per se." He sat up, scrubbing his hands through his hair as the closest thing to a plan he'd come up with all night started to reveal itself.

"What does that mean?" In the early-morning light, he could clearly see the skepticism written all over her face.

"Think about it. A man like Ballard surrounds himself with a lot of people to do his dirty work. He thinks it keeps him safe, but what it does is leave him vulnerable. Because those people have weak-nesses, and they're more likely to leave their weak-nesses where a person with your skills can find them. They don't have the resources he does."

"So we look them up, instead." A smile began to dawn. "Of course."

"I knew you'd understand." He got out of bed, eager to get started. That was always the way. Once a path showed itself, he couldn't wait to move.

Claire wasn't so eager. "Where would we start?"

"Personally, I'd like to know more about those detectives who made it their mission to trail me and my brothers, Fisher and Arellano. One or both of them have to be in bed with Ballard, which means he's either holding something over their heads or giving them money—again, because he'd know they need it for some reason. Which means you'd be able to find what he found. I know you can."

"I'm glad you have that much confidence in me," she said. "What if he has people monitoring their accounts or whatever, in case I go looking around?"

"What if he does?" Luke knelt beside the bed, taking her hands in his.

She drew a deep breath. "Right. Of course. I know how to be careful."

"I know you do."

Her shoulders squared and her jawline hardened. When she spoke, her voice was firm. "I can't be afraid of what might happen. I only need to be prepared for it."

He couldn't have loved her more. "Exactly." He kissed the backs of her hands before standing. "I know you can do it. You have what it takes. And once you've dug up all that information, you can give it to me and the boys. We'll know what to do from that point."

His brothers needed to know about this. He padded down to the kitchen to fix coffee—if ever there was a morning when he'd needed it—and once the aroma began to fill the air, he pulled out the burner phone he'd been using to keep in touch with them.

"I was just going to call you." Brax's voice was

like a snarl. That, paired with the early time of the day, made Luke's palms go slick with nervous sweat.

"What's up?" He looked up the stairs, wondering if he should let Claire overhear this.

"We're not sure… Keep that in mind. We don't have proof."

"Talk to me," Luke barked as quietly as he could. "Stop dancing around it."

A heavy sigh. "Dad called. Mom had trouble with her brakes."

Luke gripped the counter as hard as he could, forcing himself to process this without giving in to emotion. Emotion was the enemy at a time like this. "And what happened? How is she?"

"She's fine. She was smart enough to pull off the road and call for help the second she felt something was wrong."

Luke exhaled. "But no proof."

"No proof. Still, it seems—"

"A little too convenient? Yeah, it does." He muttered a string of profanity under his breath. If he had Ballard in front of him just then, what he wouldn't do to that snake.

"Chance is going to stay with them for the time being, just as a precaution."

"Good," Luke agreed. "I know it'll make me feel better knowing they have protection. And Mom will love the opportunity to stuff Chance full of her cooking, so it's sort of a win-win."

Brax chuckled. "Yeah, it's just a shame about the circumstances. What are we going do about this guy?

He's smart. He knows there has to be a connection between us and Claire, even if he can't find it. He's starting to get desperate with these so-called accidents."

"It just so happens that's why I was calling you. I have an idea that has the possibility of becoming a plan."

"I'm all ears."

Claire started down the stairs, locking eyes with him. She must have seen his troubled look for what it was, because her smile faded.

"I have a better idea," he offered. "Why don't I catch you up on it in person?"

Her chin trembled only once, enough to remind him how scared she was in spite of everything. Then she nodded. Stronger. The way he needed them to be for both their sakes.

It was time to go home.

Chapter Nineteen

Luke Patterson had done a lot of difficult things in his life.

His time in the service hadn't exactly been a cake-walk.

Even before then, when he was a kid, he'd survived a lot of situations that might have broken somebody without his strength or determination. He hadn't exactly seen it that way at the time—adulthood had a way of casting things in a different light. All he'd known back then was survival.

Yet as he drove away from the safe house where he'd stashed Claire with Weston keeping watch, he was sure he'd never done anything harder. Not even close.

"You know she's in safe hands with me," Weston had reminded him, only partly kidding around. He understood what Claire meant, how Luke felt, and what it did to him to leave her behind. Safe hands or not.

None of them would ever be satisfied with letting others protect the ones they loved, no matter who those others were.

If it wasn't for the need to put in face time around the office, he would never have considered leaving her side, no matter how remote her location. It wasn't like the cabin, in that the cabin hadn't been deliberately rigged to keep it off the grid.

This safe house was. Luke and his brothers used the cabin's generator and solar panels as inspiration to keep clients as protected as possible by making them as invisible as possible.

Even having set up the safe house himself wasn't enough to make leaving any easier. But facts were facts, and Ballard wouldn't be satisfied without confirmation of Luke being in the area and following his normal routine.

Which was why he drove to the office with his hands gripping the wheel tight enough that he could've sworn he heard the thing creak from the strain. It was why he stopped off for coffee and a bagel, making sure to take his time getting in and out of the car so anybody driving past could see him easily.

Brax was waiting at the office. "No bagel for me?"

"Here. You can have this one. I'm not hungry." He handed the bag to his brother before heading to his desk. The absence of files was still a minor miracle and enough to make him smile for a second.

"You've got to take care of yourself if you plan to take care of her." Brax leaned against the doorjamb, picking at the cinnamon raisin bagel but watching Luke all the while.

"I realize that. But I couldn't swallow a bite right

now if you paid me, not since we talked this morning." He couldn't shake the mental image of his mother realizing there was something wrong when her foot pressed down on the brake pedal and nothing happened. If she had been on the freeway—

He shook himself free of this. It was enough that she was safe. He'd drive himself insane if he kept asking "what if."

"You think Claire will be able to find what we're looking for without being noticed?"

That much he was sure of. "Absolutely. She knows what she's doing. It's one thing to not get around safeguards placed specifically to keep her out of Passage Digital's network without raising a red flag, but Ballard's people can't put up blocks to other sites not under their control. So as long as she uses her tricks to mask who she is and where she's accessing the information from, she'll be fine."

"You sound pretty confident."

"I am. She's the best. And it isn't like she doesn't understand the stakes."

"I wasn't trying to insult her. Don't get your feathers ruffled." Brax flashed one of his winning smiles, the same smile that he'd used to get out of trouble more times than Luke could count. "Just remind me once things calm down for good to make fun of you until I run out of breath for finally falling for a woman."

"I'll do that right after I remind you to grow up. How's that sound?"

His burner phone rang. Brax grew serious as he perched on the edge of Luke's desk to listen in. "Yes?" Luke answered, glancing at his brother.

"All's well," Weston assured him. "Your lady is working her fingers to the bone over here. I don't think I've ever heard keys clicking so fast."

Like that was what he wanted to hear about. "Has she found anything?"

"Oh, definitely. She hacked the security footage around the office building—not in Ballard's offices, mind you, but the ones nearby. That way he won't know somebody's been looking around. She managed to pick up clear shots of a pair of big guys who tag along with him wherever he goes. You can plainly see them from a camera across the street getting in and out of his car. She ran a facial recognition scan, and their names are Nick Masters and David Brooks—both ex-CIA, both with filthy records."

"A perfect resource for a man with no scruples."

"Exactly."

"What about those detectives? Anything there?"

"Claire is working on them as we speak. I'd guess they'll be easier to get to than these two psycho meatheads. The odds of catching one of them without Ballard nearby is greater. They're regular guys…detectives, probably with wives and kids."

"So their pressure points will be closer to the surface. Easier to find and use against them."

"Correct again. You'll get the hang of this yet."

"Everybody's a comedian all of a sudden."

There was noise in the background, making Luke's heart clench. The sound of her voice did that to him, the longing he couldn't shake. Wanting to have her there, with him, where he could see and touch her and know she was okay.

"She found something," Weston murmured. "Let's see."

"What is it?" Luke exchanged another glance with Brax, whose eyebrows were lifted high enough to practically blend in with his hairline.

"Oh. Oh, this is good. This works in our favor." Weston's dark chuckle was punctuation at the end of that statement. "I'll let the lady tell you what we're looking at."

Moments later, Claire's voice washed over Luke like a gentle rain. Just the sound of it helped him breathe easier.

She launched straight into her report. "Looks like our friendly neighborhood detective has a bad habit. There are two mortgages on Arellano's house, and he's in credit card debt up to his eyeballs."

"What is it? Drugs, drinking, women?"

"Judging by the locations of these ATM transactions, I'd say gambling."

Brax shook his head and let out a low whistle while Luke pressed on. "Any sign of interference?"

"A big flashing red sign. Man, the guy even took an early withdrawal from his IRA. His checking account was nearly in the negative. But suddenly…poof! A whole bunch of money showed up across a number of different accounts like a benevolent fairy waved a wand."

"How much?"

"There's a lot of zeroes. Let's put it that way."

"They weren't even sneaky about it."

"Eh, they were pretty sneaky," she chuckled, "but I'm sneakier."

He grinned. "Of course. I can't forget that."

"I'd say he's your way in. From what I'm seeing, Fisher is just plain dirty. He's been written up for excessive force a half dozen times in four years and has a string of citations for other offenses. How does he even have a job?"

"Somebody's convinced somebody else to look the other way," Luke decided. "How about Arellano's record?"

"Clean as a whistle."

"He's our way in, then." Luke offered Brax a smirk. "Let's see how Detective Arellano feels when the tables are turned and he's the one being tailed."

It was early evening by the time they found him, his car parked outside a Chinese take-out restaurant a few miles from the rancher he and his wife called home. There were no kids in the picture, but that didn't make him any less vulnerable—not with a gambling habit like his.

With Brax keeping lookout, Luke waited in a narrow alley between the restaurant and the dry cleaner next door. It wasn't more than a few minutes before a man in a rumpled suit emerged holding a plastic bag in one hand.

Detective Brandon Arellano wasn't at the top of his game, not even close. Luke was able to grab him and steer him toward the alley without even a hint of force. He wondered if the guy was fully aware of what was happening to him. It wasn't until they were standing face-to-face that the detective blinked hard, shaking his head a little. "Oh. It's just you."

Luke blinked, a little thrown by this reaction. "Who did you expect, Detective?"

"Not you. What are you doing?" Arellano looked back and forth, up and down the cramped passage. "Are you insane, trying to pressure me like this?"

"Who said anything about pressuring? I thought we might have a little chat, is all. You've been so interested in my life as of late, it seemed rude not to be interested in yours."

It was then that Luke noticed something.

The man looked like death warmed over, as Sheila Patterson was prone to saying. Even in the few days since Luke had last known the displeasure of the man's presence, Arellano had lost weight. The buttoned collar of his shirt was loose around his neck, his Adam's apple sticking out more prominently than before. He hadn't shaved in at least two days, and his eyes were ringed in dark circles. "What happened to you, man?" Luke asked, dropping any pretense of threat.

"It's none of your business. And if I were you—"

"You aren't me. For one, I don't look like somebody reanimated my corpse. What's going on? Don't pretend everything's fine because I know things about you. And something tells me I'm not the only one."

"What's that supposed to mean?"

"Read the racing form lately?"

Arellano's already pale skin turned ashen. "That's none of your business."

"Listen to me." Luke lowered his brow along with his voice, locking eyes with the detective. The man was terrified, sweat rolling down his face and neck. It was time to take a calculated risk. "I know Ballard's blackmailing you."

The risk paid off. Arellano's eyes flew open wide in time with the dropping of his jaw. "Wh-what?"

"You heard me. It doesn't have to be this way. The man is a disease, isn't he? He finds your weak spot and works his way in. So, what is it? He found out about your gambling and threatened to spill to the department? I mean, they can't have a degenerate gambler on the force, now, can they?"

"Watch it," Arellano snarled. "You have no idea what you're talking about."

"Don't I? I have the feeling I'm right. Call it instinct or the way your body language is taking to me. You're scared out of your wits, man. Like I said, it doesn't have to be this way."

It was clear the man didn't want to buckle. He wanted to stay strong and pretend he didn't have the first clue what Luke referred to, but there were limits to a man's resolve.

He leaned against the wall with a heavy sigh. "You're right. He found out about the gambling and threatened to go the captain unless I agreed to play along. I mean, what was I supposed to do? It seemed like the answer to a prayer. Only…" He averted his eyes.

"Only you didn't want to play along once you figured out what that would involve?"

A single nod. "Fisher…he's a complicated man. He doesn't, uh, care much about going by the book. I didn't know that Ballard already knew him, though. Not until this whole thing started. And I didn't know how far he was willing to go. I couldn't do the things Ballard wanted us to do." He shuddered, shaking his head.

Luke fought to put things together. He looked down at the bag Arellano still carried and noticed how light it looked. The condition of his clothes, the sweat stain around his collar, the stain on his tie.

An even uglier picture started to come together.

"You told him you wouldn't play his game," he murmured, "so he forced your hand."

"He took my wife. He *took* her." There were tears in the man's eyes when they met Luke's again, and the pain in his voice was almost enough to stir sympathy. "He's going to kill her if I don't see this through. I believe him."

Luke muttered a curse, hands linked on top of his

head. This was worse than any of them had imagined. "We can get you out of this."

Arellano let out a miserable laugh. "You can't believe that. Not knowing what you know, Patterson. You don't seem like a stupid person."

"You're right, I'm not. Which is why I know we can get all of us out of this, but we've got to be smart. Which means you've got to play on our team from now on."

"Don't you get it?" Arellano snarled like a trapped animal—which, in essence, was what he was. "It's quid pro quo. Claire's life for Amanda's. He wants Claire Wallace dead. He requires it, or else Amanda dies."

Luke looked away as the man started to cry, both sorry for him and more than a little uncomfortable. "He's not a disease... He's the devil incarnate."

"He is. I wish I'd known. I swear, I didn't know. I wouldn't have accepted his deal if I thought Amanda would get roped into it. She's innocent. She didn't even know about the blackmail money. I don't know where he has her—" His voice lifted in pitch, taking on a note of panic.

Luke took Arellano by the shoulders and shoved him against the cold brick wall to shake him out of his spiraling. "Okay, all right. You've gotta stay calm and rational for Amanda's sake. And you have to accept help when it comes your way. This isn't like before. I'm not Ballard. I'm not trying to trick you. There's a way we can all get what we need, but we have to work together. You need us, and we need you."

Arellano took a few deep, shuddery breaths before pulling himself together, standing straighter than before. "You said you have a plan?"

"I do."

"And this is a Ballard-proof plan?"

"Only if I have your full cooperation."

He nodded, firm now. "Okay, Patterson… Let's hear it."

Chapter Twenty

If there was anything Claire knew for sure about herself, it was that she was no hero.

She sure hadn't been one the day of Julia's murder, had she? She sat there and let it happen, watching in mute horror with her knuckles in her mouth to hold back a scream. Running like a scared rabbit afterward, barely keeping herself from breaking into a run. Not exactly heroic.

She hadn't been heroic in the days since then, either. If anything, Luke was the hero. He kept her safe, took care of her, made sure she didn't starve or set up camp under the freeway with a cat who thought he was a dog as her only friend and protector.

He had even come up with this absolutely insane plan.

She was no hero—not then, not now. And for better or worse, she was still in possession of her wits, which meant she was scared to death. Any sane person would be. So many things could go wrong.

Yet it was the only way. That was the cherry on top of a melted sundae. This plan of Luke's—crazy though it might've been—was the only way out of the madness.

Her heart pounded hard enough to make her sick; her hands were slick with sweat. She clutched the steering wheel tighter, pressing down on the gas pedal. Her poor car was just about at its limit now, its engine whining as dust kicked up behind the wheels. She sped along through the outskirts of San Antonio, just like she was supposed to.

And she had never felt lonelier in her life.

Focus. Breathe.

This had to go off cleanly. There couldn't be any doubt.

Ballard had to believe she was no longer a threat, which meant making him believe what was about to go down. She had to sell it.

"You okay?"

Brax's voice was in her ear and it brought her a measure of peace. A sliver, anyway. But it was better than nothing. "Define okay," she replied with a shaky laugh.

"You're doing great. You've got this. Just follow the plan and we're home free."

"Right." She forced herself to breathe again when she noticed she'd been holding her breath. Her entire body was tensed tight enough to hurt. This was only the beginning of things, so she had to calm down if she was going to get through it.

"We went through all this last night, right?" Brax was warm. Calm. Encouraging. He had that way about him, she noticed. His personality complemented those of his brothers. He was a sweetheart, a charmer. "You can go through the steps backward and forward."

"Right."

"Just live it out the way we planned. You know what you're doing."

"I hope that's the case when the time comes for the next step…"

"You wanna know something I've learned?"

"Please." Anything to distract her from the doubts circling her head like water circling a drain.

"You can't think too far ahead when you're in the middle of acting out a plan. You can only focus on the step you're on and pull it off the best you can. Think too much about what'll happen next and you'll mess up what you're trying to do right now."

"Got it. That makes sense." For instance, it wouldn't do her any good to run the car off the road, would it? She focused on her driving while doing her best to make it look like she was trying to get away.

If anybody had ever told her she'd end up being pursued by the cops one day, she would've laughed herself sick. Meek little Claire Wallace, who'd never said boo to a ghost? Who carried spiders outside rather than kill them outright? Why would the police have any reason to chase her?

Life had a funny way of making the impossible real. Tangible. Nauseating.

"The bridge is coming up," Brax reminded her. As if she needed the reminder. It took effort to bite back a snarky comment, which of course, would've been the result of fear. "You know what to do."

"I do." She pushed the car harder, forcing it to speeds it had probably never reached before. If anything, driving fast and being dangerous was a treat. She had spent her whole life playing it safe, keeping her head down, avoiding notice.

To think, it took the threat of being murdered to make her life a little more interesting. "All things being equal, I liked life the way it was."

"What?" Brax's soft chuckle rang through her earpiece.

"Never mind."

The San Antonio River sparkled up ahead, a ribbon cutting through the otherwise dusty, empty land outside the city. It would keep flowing south from the springs where it originated, eventually hooking up with the Guadalupe River miles downstream.

She approached the drawbridge with her heart hammering, her breath coming sharp and fast. A glance at the clock on the dash told her they were right on schedule. Everything was going according to plan, right down to the exact time she'd reach the bridge.

And down to the car speeding her way from the other side of the river.

"Here they come." She knew Brax could see them but felt the need to say it anyway. "I think my heart's going to explode."

"I promise you, it won't. Just stay the course. You can do this. You can do anything. You've made it this far, and you can keep going." Did he know how tense he sounded? How close his voice was to sliding into a bark? She probably didn't sound much better.

The tires hit the metal bridge and made an almost earsplitting noise at this speed, but she kept going. This was it. There was no going back. Might as well put on a show.

She made it roughly three-quarters of the way over the bridge before the approaching car cut her off, skidding to a stop sideways across the other end, blocking her way through.

Claire slammed her foot on the pedal and the brakes shrieked. Her body pressed against the belt hard enough to take her breath away, but that was only a thought in the background of her mind.

"Okay. On my count. Five…four…three…two… one."

Claire took a deep breath before she threw the car into Reverse and backed away from the car blocking hers, which she knew held Detectives Fisher and Arellano.

Only there was no time to get away. The drawbridge started to raise behind her, cutting her off in that direction, too. She was out of options. Her heart would surely give out on her by the time this was over, wouldn't it? It had to. She couldn't stand the strain.

Even if all of this was going exactly according to plan, exactly according to schedule. "It's going perfectly," Brax reminded her. "You're doing great. Time to move to the next step."

Right. So easy. How would he feel if he were the

one about to do what she had to do? Would he sound so calm and reassuring if he was in her place?

"Claire. You have to move." He didn't sound so calm now. He was downright demanding. "Go. Now."

Her hands fumbled with the buckle while the detectives got out of their car. She had to remind herself that Arellano knew what was happening. He was in on it.

Could they trust him? That was what made her hands so sweaty, sliding off the handle when she first tried to open the door. "Don't forget your earpiece!" Brax shouted, and she was glad he did. She plucked it from her ear and dropped it into her pocket before she opened the door and stepped out of the car.

This was it. This was for all the marbles.

Luke, please help me.

"Hands in the air!" Fisher bellowed, leveling his gun at her. Moonlight glinted off the metal. Her hands shook as she raised them, her gaze darting over to his partner. This was not the time for a trigger-happy cop to get ahead of himself.

"Stand down," Arellano ordered. "I've got this." Claire could only hope he was right, that Fisher wasn't as desperate to shut her up. She let out a shuddery breath when he holstered his weapon.

But that didn't mean she was out of the woods.

She crept closer to the edge of the bridge where a low railing was all that stood between her and the water. Was it cold? Was it rushing fast? She could only hope not.

Make sure you go to the side of the bridge facing

upstream. Right. This would all fall apart if she made a stupid, tiny mistake.

"I know you're working for him!" she called out. At least her voice sounded strong, like she wasn't quite as terrified as she felt. "Ballard. I know he has you both in his pocket. That's why you're doing this."

"Keep your hands in the air!" Arellano was either serious about wanting to stop her or he was a very good actor. Wouldn't that be the ultimate kick in the head—a double-cross on a double-cross?

What if he'd been lying the whole time? What if there was nothing wrong with his wife? What if Ballard had him tell that story to make himself seem sympathetic? To lure them into a trap?

No. There was no room for doubt. She had to believe. She had to trust the plan.

Arellano shook his head with a stern expression. "You don't know what you're talking about!"

One step closer to the railing. Another step. Her knees threatened to buckle. She couldn't let that happen. That would ruin everything. "I do!" she shouted, and she let her heartache and disappointment and fear come out. And her disgust—deep, pulsing, bile-flavored disgust. "You're in this with him! You accepted his dirty money, his promises, and look where it got you! This is wrong! You know it is! I didn't do anything wrong! I never killed anybody—he's the killer, not me!"

"Just stop talking," Fisher warned. "This doesn't have to end badly for you. But it does have to end. You can't run from the police forever. Your best bet is

to come with us, Claire. You said you didn't do anything. You have no reason to run."

The railing was within her reach. Did she have to
guts to do this? Well, she'd had the guts to do everything else so far. This was just one more thing she
would never have imagined before now, not in her
wildest dreams.

"You're lying!" Was she laughing? It seemed un-
thinkable. There was nothing funny about this. But
there were all sorts of reasons for a person to laugh.
Like when a situation was beyond the absurd, which
applied to this situation.

The water was just below her, rushing audibly. Or
was that the blood rushing in her ears? If only Luke
was here with her. If only she could hear Brax's voice
again, but keeping the earpiece in was dangerous. Not
only because one of the men at the end of the bridge
might see it. The last thing she needed was for the
thing to short out while in her ear.

"Come with us and you'll see." Fisher's voice was
deceptively quiet, bringing to mind a snake. That was
what he was, too. A snake in the grass, lying in wait.
Lying in general, in fact. She almost laughed again.

"I don't think so. I don't think I'll make it to the
police station. Isn't that right, Detective?" She looked
at Arellano, willing him to go along with what was
supposed to happen next. Everything hinged on what
was about to happen next. He had to sell this just as
much as she did—more than she did. In another few
moments, her part would be over.

"Just come with us, Claire," he shouted. "This can

all be finished. But you have to stop running. We're not the only people looking for you."

"You think I don't know that?" Her hip bumped the railing. This was it. Everything would come down to this. She stiffened her spine against the fear threatening to break her. "But Ballard wants me dead. Stop pretending he doesn't. Stop lying for him!"

"Claire…"

"Have a little courage!" she screamed. "A little integrity! How do you sleep at night, doing what you do for him? You cowards! You filthy, lying, murdering—"

"Enough!"

Arellano's deep, bellowing voice mixed with the sharp, sudden crack of a gunshot.

Oh, Luke. Help me.

Claire closed her eyes and went over the railing, into the dark water below.

Chapter Twenty-One

It was like watching a horror movie unfold in slow motion. Only this was too real.

Claire's limp body seemed to float through the air, falling, falling. How could it take so long for someone to fall off a bridge? It wasn't such a long drop—they'd chosen that particular bridge not only because it sat in an empty area, but because the drop wasn't so far. Hence, it being a drawbridge, too low for anything to pass underneath without it opening.

He braced himself for impact almost like it was his body about to hit the water. It might as well have been. Claire was his life, nothing less than everything that mattered.

She hit the river with a splash, roughly where they'd worked out her impact. Close to where he was waiting under the bridge. He waited a second before letting go of the dummy dressed in clothes identical to Claire's, floating it facedown.

He then ducked under the surface, taking hold of Claire before the river's current pulled her out of reach. She was panicked, struggling against him even though everything was going according to plan. He guided the mouthpiece to her lips, his scuba gear allowing him to breathe underwater. She had to breathe, too.

And she could once she settled down and let him insert the device into her mouth. She clung to him the way he clung to her with all his might. She was safe. She would be okay.

She was, after all, dead.

Well, not exactly. Thanks to the blank Arellano had fired and the dummy Luke had set loose, to Fisher it would look like Claire was out of commission and no longer a threat. With the report coming from both detectives, Ballard would have no choice but to believe she was dead.

Now all they had to do was wait, holding on to each other beneath the water's surface. He could just make out beams of light shining down from the bridge. Flashlights. Arellano probably wanted to make sure his partner saw the lifeless dummy before it rounded the bend and floated out of sight.

It was a long fifteen minutes, with Luke keeping watch on the riverbank and waiting for the signal. When a bright light flashed from inside the trees, he knew they were in the clear. Brax had been keeping watch and was satisfied that both cars were gone. They'd made sure to leave no trace of Claire in her car. Just the keys, so one of the men could drive it off the bridge and somehow make it disappear.

They'd wipe out all memory of Claire's existence. At least, that was what Ballard would believe.

Or so they hoped.

Luke pulled Claire to the surface with him where she tore the respirator from her mouth and gulped fresh air. "I can't believe it worked," she whispered, her teeth chattering.

"You don't trust me now, Kitten?" He tried to keep his voice light and teasing. Like it was completely normal for them to take a swim in the river in the middle of the night. For her to pretend she'd been shot and pitch herself off the side of the bridge.

God, how he loved her. Her strength and courage. He wasn't even sure whether he'd have the guts to throw himself off a bridge, no matter whether the fall had been planned or not.

He held on to her as he swam for shore, where Brax waited with a car and towels. "You were perfect," Brax whispered, wrapping one of the towels around Claire while Luke pulled off his goggles and slid the oxygen tank off his back. "I told you so."

"You told me." Her voice was shaky, though it was clear she was trying to sound cheerful and relieved. And she had every right to be relieved—she'd cheated death.

"Let's get you back to the house." Luke guided her into the back seat of Brax's car, noting the way she shivered until her teeth chattered. He had a feeling there was more to it than feeling chilly, still soaked from the river. He made a point of holding her close while Brax drove, trying to warm her, trying to comfort her.

Sure, she was out of the worst of it. Safe, now that

Ballard thought she was dead. That didn't mean the enormity of what she'd just done wouldn't hit her from all sides. The thought of what might've gone wrong. What if Fisher had fired on her instead? He didn't have the first clue what was happening, that his partner had gone into business with the enemy to save his wife's life.

Would she be safe now? Luke hoped so. He didn't hold anything against the guy for getting himself trapped in the spider's web. Ballard knew how to choose his prey, how to wrap them up so they couldn't escape.

"You're sure they won't find the dummy?" Claire lifted her head from his shoulder, looking up at him with eyes that seemed a lot bigger than usual.

"They won't. It'll end up in the Guadalupe before long, and from there, it'll sail into the Gulf. It'll be enough for them to hide or destroy the car, so there won't be any trace of you lying around. By the time that's finished, the dummy will be gone for good. Nothing to worry about."

"I hope you're right..." She wanted to believe him, he knew she did. Though the fact that there was any doubt didn't exactly thrill him.

He guessed he'd be afraid to bask in victory if Ballard had burned him so many times. Not only Ballard—life had burned Claire again and again for years. No wonder she was hesitant to rest easy.

If he had his way, that would never happen again.

"So, what now?" Claire's head found his shoulder and she let out a soft sigh while she snuggled in.

He stroked her wet hair, still heavy with the smell of the river.

"First, we shower."

She snickered. "I thought that went without saying."

"Then, we settle you in so you can get some sleep. You can't burn the candle at both ends forever. We spent all last night going over the plan. Clearly, the effort was worth it. Now you need to sleep."

"You know I appreciate how much you care about me, right?"

"Right." He sensed there was something more to it than that.

"But I don't need you to tell me to rest. I know I need to sleep. I wasn't talking about this very night. What's our next move?"

Brax met his gaze in the mirror, eyes crinkling at the corners. He could afford to smile, couldn't he? Claire wasn't the love of his life. If they were still kids, that little grin would've earned Brax a punch in the arm.

A punch in the arm sounded good right about then, all things considered.

"Can't it be enough for now to rest and regroup?" he asked Claire in a softer voice than before. "You faked your death not forty-five minutes ago. If anything you've ever done has earned you the right to unplug for a minute and recharge, it's what you just pulled off."

She went silent, which he wasn't sure was a good sign. His mom would go silent like that whenever she was good and frustrated with his dad.

Which was why he didn't push Claire to answer.

The ride to the safe house felt like it took years, thanks to the roundabout route Brax followed to get them there. "Just in case," he muttered more than once, taking them down unlit roads, sometimes doubling back. Once he felt comfortable there was no one on their tail, he took them the rest of the way to the safe house.

It was dark and empty. Weston and Chance had made it their business to be seen around town earlier in the evening prior to settling in at home—well before Claire had played out her one-act drama with Detective Arellano—just in case Ballard had been watching for signs of life from them.

Brax entered first, checking for any signs of trouble before waving them in. Luke hurried Claire up to the front door, an arm around her waist, his head on a swivel. They couldn't be too careful, even now.

Once they were inside and he could see for himself that all was well, he allowed himself to breathe. No one could ever call him lazy or out of shape, yet the events of the evening had left him with a bone-deep exhaustion now that the rush of adrenaline had tapered off.

"You okay?" Brax asked while Claire went to shower off the river's stench. The frown lines creasing his brow revealed his concern.

"Fine. Glad that's over, for sure." Luke opened a bottled water and downed half in one desperate go, signaling dehydration. "Is it possible to sweat bullets while you're underwater?"

"You were worried about her."

"No kidding. Of course, I was. It was the longest few minutes of my life between her rolling onto the bridge and falling off."

"She's gutsy, I'll give her that. She held up under pressure." Brax elbowed him, and a little of his usual good humor flashed in his smile. "You chose well."

Brax couldn't understand, so Luke didn't bother to explain the finer details. There had been no choice involved. Life had put them together, and something about Claire had spoken to something inside him. Maybe his protective nature sensed someone in serious need of someone like him.

Rather than try to explain, he stripped off his wetsuit and ducked into the shower once Claire was finished. Her skin was pink, like she'd scrubbed it within an inch of its life. He couldn't blame her. Even though he'd been covered while underwater, he soaped up twice and rinsed in water as hot as he could stand before stepping out.

He found her sitting on the bed, combing her hair, and his heart swelled with love and relief. Was this how it would always be? Every time he saw her, even if she were engaged in something so commonplace, would he have this same reaction? He hoped not, on reflection, since he planned on their lives being very dull and ordinary once Ballard was out of commission. He wouldn't carry the constant fear of losing her.

"In case I didn't make it clear to you before now, you were amazing." He dried off and dressed quickly before he sat next to her. "You couldn't have done any better out there. I hope it doesn't come off as conde-scension when I tell you how proud you make me."

Her hand closed over his. "You don't sound con-descending at all. I'm just glad it's over and I don't have to dread faking my death anymore."

Rather than give him time to draw her into his arms, she all but jumped up from the bed. "I know how to finish this."

Luke barely held back his surprise at this sudden announcement—and the absolute dead-eyed certainty with which she delivered it. "You do?"

She gave a single, firm nod. "I do. I've been toss-ing the idea around in my head like a computer pro-gram running in the background while we worked out the plan for tonight." She managed a faint smile.

"Okay. What's the idea?" There was an intensity in the way she moved, the hard glint in her eyes. As much as he wished he could take away any reason for her to look and act that way, there was no deny-ing how proud she made him. Her ingenuity, her ca-pability, her courage.

"Ballard loves nothing more than feeling secure, right?" She didn't pause for an answer, rolling on through. "He finds people to do his dirty work for him. He has eyes everywhere, reporting back to him. He wraps himself in layers of firewalls and cameras and monitoring, like he's protected against the en-tire world."

"Only a man who poses a threat to the entire world needs to go to those lengths," Luke mused.

Claire nodded. "Exactly. And it's all an illusion.

It takes nothing more than a person with awareness of how he does things and the skill to get around his defenses to take him down."

"You're the person with the awareness and the skill."

"I am." She raised her chin like she dared him to argue, but he wouldn't have argued for anything in the world.

"What does that mean?"

"I'm going to use his security system against him. Against all of them."

Chapter Twenty-Two

Whatever special something Brax Patterson had, he could've made a mint from bottling and selling it.

"I told you he'd come through." Luke grinned once his brother had confirmed success on the first step of this latest part of their plan. What would be the end of everything, if it all played out the way they needed it to.

No. The way *she'd* make it play out. It was all in her hands now, and Claire could almost taste victory. So long as Ballard kept acting predictably, she'd be fine. And if there was one thing she'd finally started to understand about Ballard, it was his lack of imagination.

Anyone could've predicted what he'd done so far, if they were willing to sink to his level and think like a power-hungry, greedy sociopath.

Her one advantage over him so far was that total lack of imagination. He hadn't imagined her to be strong, smart or capable. He'd looked at her—or through her the way so many people had all her life— and seen nothing. Nobody.

Talk about a blow to his ego. How much of his desperation to find her stemmed from his fear of what she could do to him and how much came from his crushed pride?

Luke switched on the burner phone's speaker. "You got it?" Claire asked. Khan took this as an invitation to leap into her lap, wanting all her attention as always.

She kissed the top of his head anyway. He was her spoiled brat.

"I got it." It was clear Brax was smiling, proud of himself. "It was easier than I thought. The ladies at that company need to get laid. She was too glad to stop and chat with me for a little while on her way to her car."

Claire rolled her eyes. "Or maybe you're the most charming devil who ever lived and whoever she was, she couldn't help but fall under your spell."

"Stop. You're making me blush."

Luke snickered. "Okay, okay. Back to business. You have the key card, which means we have access to the building tonight. Weston secured the new laptop and is on his way with it. Claire knows what to do when she gets her hands on it."

She nodded her agreement while wondering how true that was. There she went again, doubting herself when she'd been so sure, so completely certain. She saw it all clearly, each step, everything she had to do.

All that was left was actually doing it.

Weston had followed her instructions to the letter, finding a machine with the capabilities she was looking for. The power she needed, the speed. Speed would be their weapon. When the ball started rolling, it would have to roll fast.

And she'd be the one pushing it along.

The hardest part might very well have been waiting to get started. At least there was one task to keep her occupied—hacking into the security feed.

"You're sure you won't be noticed?" Luke leaned in behind her, squinting at the screen.

"This is the least of our worries, believe me. Nobody considers a hack to their security cameras—and even if they do, they expect the hack to shut down the system. I'm not shutting it down. I'm looping the same twenty minutes on repeat, so it looks like nothing out of the ordinary is going down while we go to work."

"While you go to work, you mean."

She took a second to kiss his cheek before turning back to the security feed. "You're too sweet. We both know darn well you'll be working, too." No way would she walk into the building alone. Even if she had the nerve to go in on her own, Luke wouldn't allow it.

"If you do your job fast, there won't be anything to do on my end. I'll be downright bored."

She withheld her comment. It was nice to imagine things going smoothly, but a beaten dog still flinched when a hand came its way, even if it hadn't been beaten in a long time.

It hadn't been too long since Ballard had killed people who used to mean a lot to Claire.

She couldn't shake the pit of fear in her stomach when she imagined Ballard taking the person who meant the most.

For his sake, she kept a positive attitude—on the outside, at least.

It was after midnight by the time they rolled out, taking two cars. She rode with Luke and Weston, while Brax and Chance took the second vehicle. If anything went south, it was better to have two cars involved, so whoever was in a position to flee might be able to.

However, she strongly doubted any one of the four Patterson brothers would leave any of the others behind. They might not have shared blood, but they were brothers in every other respect.

This would be the last time she'd ever visit Passage Digital. Rolling into the adjoining parking garage was like stepping back in time, reminding her of better days. She might never have exactly been thrilled to work here—it was always a means to an end, a stepping-stone, a paycheck—but life had been much less complicated then.

And lonelier. There was no Luke back then. He'd been nothing more than a memory.

In the end, it seemed like a fair trade-off.

"You ready?" He put the car in Park and turned to look at her. The hard set of his jaw and narrowed eyes spoke to his strain and his worry for her.

The least she could do was stiffen her spine. "Yes. I'm ready." She carefully slung the pack onto her back, knowing Khan didn't like being jostled around too hard. He'd already been through enough, the poor thing. They both had.

"You sure it was a good idea to bring him?" Weston asked in his "concerned dad" voice. He was such a cop.

Luke knew better. "There's no separating those two. She'd sooner leave me at home than she would that cat-dog hybrid of hers." She smiled, but didn't bother correcting him. He wasn't entirely wrong.

They used the key card that Brax had swiped from the girl he'd flirted with earlier to access the building without setting off any alarms. Though even with the easy entrance, there was no time to dawdle.

They dashed to the elevator and picked the floors in question, planning to split up. "You have your terminal numbers and access codes?" she asked, though she knew they would. They were professionals, not about to lose something so important. Still, double-checking put her mind at ease.

Brax took one floor. Chance, the next. Weston exited after him, leaving Luke and Claire to get off the elevator on the floor she used to work on. Again, the sense of past and present overlapping threatened to overwhelm her. She took a deep breath and pushed it aside.

Luke kept watch, using his earpiece to confirm his brothers were in place and had successfully logged into their machines. "They're in," he muttered. Claire took a seat, leaving Khan and the pack under the desk. She then opened the laptop and plugged in the

precious drive she'd been guarding with her life—
the one holding the files Julia had lost her life over.

Something inside her took over. Something bigger than her, some deeper intelligence in her subconscious. So long as she could relax and trust her
instincts, she'd be fine.

It was the rest of them she worried about.

"Okay. Phase one." She clicked the button and let
the program run. Each of the computer terminals
Luke's brothers had accessed would appear to be the
ones attempting to access the network, to dig deep
into the files in which Claire had hidden the video
of Julia's murder.

Meanwhile, Luke used a tablet to monitor the building's real-time security feed rather than the loop Claire
fed to the security guards' monitors. "They're un-
aware," he reported. "Business as usual." She only
half heard him, now facing the almost impenetrable
layers of security put in place to stop her.

Almost impenetrable…but not entirely.

"Phones are cut," she whispered. "There's no communication out of the building. Radio frequencies
jammed, too." Luke reported this to his brothers,
confirming the next phase's completion. Even if the
security guards caught wind of their presence, they
wouldn't be able to call the police or request backup
from Ballard's cronies. There wouldn't be any communication among them, either.

However, there was the risk of one of them trying
to check in with another for some other reason, and
she knew it. They would probably confirm all was

well at the quarter hour and more likely at the half, and they'd know there was a problem when their radios didn't work.

It was twenty-four minutes past.

Was that sweat trickling down the back of her neck?

"How's it going?" Luke whispered behind her.

She never took her eyes from the screen. "It's going." Even if the guards caught wind of something being amiss, the Patterson brothers had log-in credentials for four terminals each and directions for where to find them. They'd already planned out their next target, and the next. The point was to keep security thinned out, running from floor to floor, chasing ghosts. Luke was watching for any approaching guards so he could give his brothers the heads-up to start moving.

He muttered a curse. "Here we go." She knew that meant security was onto them. "Chance, you need to move. Now."

Her hands flew faster than ever. They were already running out of time.

"Brax. On to your next terminal. Move."

Cold sweat ran down the back of her neck and pooled between her breasts. The progress bar inched, signaling the decryption in progress. It wasn't moving fast enough, yet she knew it would only take a minute for the process to wrap up.

Which was the longest minute of her life.

"Weston, you've got two on you, approaching from above and below." There was extra strain in Luke's voice, which was more of a sharp bark at this point. She could almost taste the fear for his brother.

Come on, come on, faster. Weston will be trapped soon.

Luke's hand cupped her shoulder. "Claire, you've gotta pause it."

"I can't. We're too close."

"I have to help Weston. I have to get them off him. They'll kill him, you know they will. I'm closest, so it has to be me."

He left the tablet on the desk next to the laptop. "Stay here. Don't move. I'll be right back, I swear." He took her by the back of the neck and silenced anything she might've said by pressing a hard, desperate kiss against her mouth.

She watched the live feed with her heart in her throat, tracking the guards closing in on Weston's floor as victory slipped through her fingers like sand.

Chapter Twenty-Three

"Come on. Come on, Luke." Claire chewed her lip hard enough to pierce the skin, watching as Luke moved between floors via the camera feed on his tablet.

This wasn't something she'd prepared for or thought out in advance.

This gut-twisting, nauseating dread.

The feeling that she was watching her life crumble in real time.

What if he got shot?

What if they killed him?

There would be nothing for her to do about it, nothing she could say. A decryption program wouldn't bring him back. Wouldn't erase the guilt. The pain. The loss.

Khan was restless in the pack at her feet. He sensed her anxiety; he always did. She couldn't find the breath to comfort him. Who was going to comfort her if she lost Luke?

And it was all her fault.

There was movement from another section of the screen, another camera's feed. Chance was on his way to his next terminal—only he'd end up on a floor where two guards currently patrolled, weapons drawn.

"No," she breathed, her heart sinking. Her stomach clenched and threatened to expel everything in it. Only the thought of Khan's reaction at being thrown up on stopped her.

She had no way of warning him. Why hadn't she thought to get an earpiece for herself? She could only watch and let things unfold. She was utterly powerless.

The same powerlessness she'd felt all her life. Every day for so long. No power. No say in how things unfolded.

And she was tired of it.

She realized there was something she could do.

Because at this point, what did it matter? If they were going to die, it had better be for a good reason.

She turned to the keyboard and clicked the key to continue the decryption program. Luke had asked her to put it on pause—for once, she shouldn't have listened to him. They were losing valuable time. Every second she wasted was one more second in which the Patterson brothers risked their lives.

If anything, starting the process again would mean drawing security away from them and toward her.

Could she stand that? Could she take that onto herself?

"Yes," she decided. "Because they're doing this for me." Khan meowed, signaling his agreement.

Every second lasted an hour. Claire's gaze darted

back and forth between the tablet and her screen. Luke had vanished from sight.

She couldn't breathe. Her lungs wouldn't take in air.

No, there he was. Darting up a flight of stairs, hugging the wall. Weston was behind him. The pressure in her chest lessened.

But they weren't out of the woods yet, not even close. *Those guards must have cloned themselves,* she decided. They were spreading everywhere.

Just another minute. Maybe two. That was all they needed.

Her head snapped up at the sound of a door closing. She held her breath. Her muscles froze, like the first few seconds after waking up from a nightmare.

Only this was no nightmare…this was very, very real. And somebody was on the floor with her.

Her head might not have moved, but her eyes did. She looked down at the tablet and could still see Luke, Weston. Chance. Brax.

It wasn't one of them.

One of the guards? There was no telling how many of them existed, so it could've been one of them. The progress bar crept so slowly. Could she stall?

Footfalls. Closer now. Tears filled her eyes, but she found the ability to move in time to knuckle them away. There was no time for tears.

What would Luke do? What would he want her to do?

She turned away from the computer with her hands

raised, blocking the screen as best she could with her body.

Her heart stopped when she saw who she was facing.

No wonder he'd moved so slowly. He'd been playing with her. Again.

"Hello, Claire." Vance Ballard flashed the sort of smile he usually saved for the media with his Mr. Good Guy persona. "You have no idea how hard I've been looking for you. How you've inconvenienced me. And I don't enjoy being inconvenienced."

"You don't look surprised to see me," she whispered. Every ounce of her wanted to look at her screen, at the tablet, but she didn't dare take her eyes off him.

Only an idiot would take their eyes off a snake when it slithered its way closer.

"That's because I'm not surprised." He came to a stop, his feet planted and arms folded. With his chin raised, he looked at her over the tip of his nose. "I didn't buy that whole fake death for even a second."

She gulped. What did that mean for Arellano's wife? And why was she worried about either of them right now? "Y-you didn't?"

Tipping his head to the side, he looked like a disappointed parent. "Oh, come on, Claire. We both know you. You aren't brave enough to face down two armed law enforcement officers without there being another plan in place. The moment those two nitwits came to me with the news, I suspected you had something up your sleeve."

"You could've come after me right away. Could've put my name back on the news, offered a larger reward—"

"No. That wouldn't do." He shook his head. "You had to believe that I believed it—which meant releasing that detective's wife, as much as I hated doing so."

At least that part had worked. "Why let her go?" she asked. "If you knew it was all a trick?"

"Detective Arellano had outlived his usefulness—and I couldn't run the risk of him alerting you. I let him leave town with his wife, let him leave and never come back. I don't care very much." He snickered. "It's not like anyone would believe his story anyway…"

Where were the guys? Where were the guards?

Where was she on the decryption?

She licked her parched lips. "We could back him up, you know."

"You won't be alive long enough to back him up, Claire." He laughed softly, but there was a hardness in his eyes. That hardness was always there. It always had been. She had only tried to ignore it back in the day when he was nothing but her boss.

He had always been empty.

"You think you're going to kill me now?" She snickered the way he had. *Let him see how good it felt to be laughed at.* "You've tried all this time… You think you'll succeed now?"

"You were stupid enough to walk in here and make it easy for me." He threw his hands into the air with a dramatic sigh. "Come on, Claire, I know you. I know everything about you. Which was why I knew you couldn't have been brave enough to face those men if you weren't absolutely certain they wouldn't kill you."

"I wasn't certain… The other one could've shot me. And the fall from the bridge could've—"

His sharp bark of laughter cut her off. "Please. A cowardly thing like you? Sure, you might take a risk to avoid capture, but we both know you would've collapsed and trembled like a leaf if you hadn't gone into that situation with at least a fair degree of certainty of your success."

Before she had the chance to tell him off, he continued, "I know everything there is to know about you. Don't you understand that by now? How did you think I was able to track down your former foster families?"

A lump lodged in her throat. She pressed her lips together to keep from letting out a sob.

The corners of his mouth twitched, and she realized he enjoyed watching her suffer in silence.

"I know your pain points. I know your weaknesses. Information is my stock-in-trade, Claire. You ought to know that by now. Isn't that what this is all about?"

"Information?"

"And the power it holds. Mind you, only the right sort of person can wield that power. Only they can take that information and turn it into something useful. Even the sharpest blade is nothing in the hands of a rube."

"I'll keep that in mind."

"You will keep nothing in mind." His playful, toying expression shifted, hardened.

He reached into the inner pocket of his suit jacket and pulled out a semiautomatic. "Though I'm glad we had this time together, Claire…really, I am. I wanted to explain myself to you before bringing an end to your useless little life."

"Useless?" She forced herself to not flinch away from the sight of the gun and maintain eye contact. "I created the program you're going to use to steal that all-powerful information you have such a craving for. How does that make me useless?"

"Because you would've left it lying there! All that knowledge. All that power. Right within your grasp, and you would've let a golden opportunity pass you by! Too concerned with honesty and integrity and all the pretty words people use to mask their weakness. Their aversion to doing what needs to be done to get them what they want."

"I didn't want that. Neither did Julia."

"Which is why you are both expendable. The world is no place for the weak, Claire. I'm only culling the herd."

She went cold when he raised the gun and leveled it at her. His hand trembled, but only slightly. He would make the shot.

Which was when the sweetest sound in the world met her ears.

The soft chime of a program reaching its conclusion.

There was no holding back her smile. "Thank you, Mr. Ballard."

His brow furrowed, his gun still pointed at her chest. "For what?"

"For giving my decryption program the time it needed to complete its job."

It was all worth it.

The terror. The running. The pain. Knowing her life could end at any time.

It was worth it just to watch the brief flash of fear wash over his face.

"You're lying." He lowered the gun but charged at her anyway, shoving her aside and bending over the laptop. "What have you done?"

"What I came here to do." She eyed the tablet, willing somebody to come. Quickly.

"Which was?"

"You knew I recorded Julia's murder." She spat the last word. "You knew somebody was watching from another terminal. I bet you tried to find the file, too. But even you couldn't manage that. But little old me…? I hid it where you'd never think to look—and even if you did, you'd never recognize it after encryption or know how to decrypt it yourself. Always using other people to make up for your inadequacies."

This was almost fun, and it might've been if the question of whether the Pattersons had survived didn't hang over her.

Whether Luke had survived.

"No. No! What have you done to it?" He pocketed the gun. His hands flew in a blur over the keys while curses poured from his mouth.

"What have I done to you, you mean?" Yes, she had strength now, the strength she'd always possessed. Only it was a lot easier to let it show while the monster in front of her fell apart.

She watched as he floundered. Nobody could ever have explained how satisfying it would be to watch him panic this way.

"I should thank you for coming up here to see me, since that was what gave me the time I needed to finish running the program. I knew once I started asking questions, you wouldn't be able to help yourself. You would have to grandstand."

"Quiet," he growled, still working and breathing hard.

"What are you trying to do? Delete the file? Destroy it? What about the external drive hooked up to the machine? It has all the files Julia sent me. All the proof of what you planned to do with our app. You should try to destroy that, too, before the information falls into the wrong hands."

He swore again. "You'll pay for this, Claire Wallace."

"You first."

He stood upright, taking a step back from the machine when the display changed.

There were now only four words on an otherwise black screen.

<Files Sent. End Program.>

"What does that mean?" His eyes were wide and oh so panicked when his head snapped around. "What did you do?"

"You did it." She jerked her chin toward the laptop. "You tripped the program I created. All you had to do was keep your hands off and there wouldn't be anything but files on that machine. Just there, nowhere else."

"And now?" he bellowed, his face red and sweat rolling down his neck.

"Now you've sent the files to the entire San Antonio Police Department."

Panic turned to horror. "No...you're bluffing."

"Julia's murder. The files she sent me with your intentions to steal data from your clients. It's all there, and now they have it."

"Lies!"

"Wait and see. I expect they'll be opening their email anytime now. It won't take long for the police to come knocking." When he only stared at her in slack-jawed surprise, she shrugged. "I know you, too, Mr. Ballard. I knew you wouldn't be able to leave well enough alone. You're the one who delivered your own death blow, you monster. I hope it was all worth it."

He shook his head as his body began to tremble. "Lying," he murmured. "Buying time."

"I'm not."

"You are."

"Just wait and see."

They stood that way for what felt like forever but might have lasted no longer than moments. Eye-to-eye. She would never forget the thrill of knowing she'd taken him down. Of watching realization begin to dawn when she didn't flinch, didn't falter.

He knew she was telling the truth.

Which was why he reached into his pocket for the gun and leveled it at her chest. "You're dead."

Chapter Twenty-Four

It had been too long.

He'd left Claire alone for far too long.

"Luke, slow down." Weston took the stairs behind him, urging him in a soft voice.

Easy for him to say. Could Weston slow it down if it meant leaving the woman he loved unguarded for even a minute?

He didn't take the time to answer; instead, he opened the door to Claire's floor and swept over the area in front of him with narrowed eyes. It looked empty, just as it had been before.

But something was different.

The air…there was a charge in it. Someone else was there, out of sight.

Claire was talking. He could just make out the sound of her voice. And while Luke wouldn't put it past her to hold a full conversation with the cat—

He took off, moving as swiftly as he was able while staying silent.

He should've known. How had he not seen this happen?

His gun was drawn; the sound of his brothers whispering in his ear as they kept track of one another's locations was mere background noise as he zeroed in on his target.

And the man who'd just aimed a gun at her chest.

"You're dead," Ballard spat.

Luke took it all in at once, all in the time it took his heart to beat.

Ballard looked like death, which was fitting considering who he was and what he'd done. Soaked in sweat, shaking, chalky.

And Claire. In spite of the semiautomatic that was now pointed at her chest, she looked...

Triumphant.

Luke mimicked Ballard's position, aiming at the man's head. He didn't want to have to go that far, especially since he didn't want to take the risk of Claire being shot, but if it meant distracting Ballard long enough to spare her life, then he'd stop at nothing.

Which, he feared, was Ballard's mode of thinking as well. He would stop at nothing to end Claire's life.

"Ballard. It's over."

Ballard turned his head just enough to take in the sight of Luke aiming at him. "You're right. It is. But not for me."

"Yes. For you." Ballard returned his gaze to Claire. "Hey, I'm talking to you," Luke barked. "Look at me, Vance."

Ballard snorted. "Don't turn that tactical knowledge on me. Using first names, trying to talk sense.

Letting me believe you're on my side, that this can all end well. We both know it won't."

"I need you to look at me, Ballard." If he felt more comfortable with last names, then so be it. "You're right. We both know this won't end well. But you'll only make it worse if you shoot her."

"Worse?" Ballard laughed—it had an edge to it, threatening to cross over into something like madness. "Worse than what? If what she told me is true and the entire police department has the files now, I'm finished. But I can at least know I made her pay. I can take that memory with me, at least."

"You wanna make her pay?" Luke glanced at Claire just long enough to take in the sight of her, trembling and wide-eyed. He didn't dare take his eyes off Ballard longer than that.

"Wouldn't you?"

"Yeah. I guess I would, if I were you. I'd want to make the person responsible for my downfall suffer for what they did to me."

"We can agree on that, then."

"But killing her isn't the answer. I'm serious," he insisted when Ballard laughed again. "You end her life, it's over. It's finished. She's gone. That's not suffering, is it?"

Ballard was silent, though the gun remained unmoving.

"Now, shooting me? Killing me? That's suffering."

"No," Claire whispered.

Luke shot her a look. This wasn't the time for her to try to be heroic.

"Are you listening, Ballard? Do you hear what I'm saying? You shoot me and she'll suffer."

"Why would she?" There was that sneer Luke had expected. "Don't tell me the two of you are in love."

"I've loved her since we were kids. You were right," Luke admitted with a sigh. "There was a connection. Thanks to a convenient name change when I was adopted, there was no way for you or your men to figure out how we knew each other. Your instincts were right on the money, though. I've loved her since we met in a foster program years ago. She remembered me and came to me for help."

"I thought so."

"Yeah, you're a smart guy." Luke looked at the gun in Ballard's hand. "I love her, and I think she might love me, too. But even if she doesn't, you know her well enough to know that she'll blame herself for the rest of her life for getting me killed. Do you see what I'm saying? Kill her now, and it's over."

Luke pointed his pistol at the ceiling, his other hand raised at shoulder-height. "Vance. Look at me."

"Don't do this!" Claire begged.

"Quiet." He maintained his focus on Ballard. It didn't matter at this point whether he aimed at the man or not. Getting a shot off at Ballard would still put Claire in danger—he might squeeze the trigger as his body reacted to being shot.

Luke could just about see the wheels turning in the man's head.

He wanted to hurt Claire; he wanted to see her suffer.

Wanted to watch her die in front of him for taking away everything he'd ever held dear. All his power. His prestige.

"Shoot me and she'll crumple like a dry leaf," Luke promised. "And let's face it, Vance. I'm just as responsible for this as she is. More so, even. If it wasn't for me, she never would've made it this far. You would've caught her long before now and put an end to this. I'm the one who hid her. I'm the one who worked the fake-out with the detectives."

"And you know what?" he concluded with a grim smile. "I loved every second of it, because it meant giving you what you deserve—making you pay for what you've done."

Ballard looked from Claire to Luke and back again.

The gun didn't move. Didn't even tremble.

It wasn't working. None of what Luke tried was working.

"Stop trying to play the hero, Patterson." Ballard snickered. "I'm not impressed with your mind games. And if you're responsible for this, then you deserve to suffer just as much as she does. I think making you watch her die before you do should be apt punishment."

"No!" Luke shouted and lunged, knowing he wouldn't be fast enough.

He wasn't fast enough.

But someone else was.

Khan.

"What the—" Ballard let out a cry of pain and surprise when claws dug into his arm. The cat had leaped from the backpack to protect his owner, latching onto Ballard's gun arm, and holding on for all he was worth.

And that was all the time Luke needed.

He threw himself at Ballard, driving him to the floor where they landed in a tangle of arms and legs.

The man barely noticed since a cat who thought he was a dog still held on tight, claws sinking through Ballard's sleeve. "Get it off! Get it off!" he screamed.

Luke pried the cat free and set him loose while he pinned Ballard to the floor. "You're finished," he spat, disgust and rage finally coming to the surface now that Claire was out of this monster's crosshairs.

"No!" Ballard struggled, still holding the gun now pinned between them. He kicked, screamed, bucked in the effort to throw Luke off him. "No, this isn't how it ends!"

Luke took hold of his wrist, pressing hard with two fingers just below the heel of his hand. No matter how a person fought to hold their grip on an object, there was no fighting that pressure point.

Ballard's hand fell open long enough for Luke to snatch the weapon away. He slid it across the floor before delivering a sharp blow to Ballard's jaw, knocking him unconscious.

It was over.

What a weak, pathetic monster he'd turned out to be.

"What do you think you're doing?" A familiar pair of thugs ran from the corner office with their guns drawn—it had to be Ballard's, Luke realized, and probably had a separate entrance. That was how he'd managed to get up here without them knowing about it.

Weston had been waiting by the stairwell all along and jumped into action, followed by Chance and Brax.

When one of the thugs aimed at Chance, Weston drove his head into the man's stomach, knocking the wind from his lungs before they both hit the floor. He took the man by the wrist and slammed his hand against the floor once, then twice, before the gun fell free.

Chance and Brax made quick work of the second attacker, who quickly realized he was no match for two skilled gunmen at once. He raised his hands, dropping his pistol. He might have even looked relieved that it was all over. Chance zip-tied him while Weston did the same with his thug.

Claire. Where was she?

Luke stood, allowing his brothers to make short work of the unconscious Ballard. He looked around, his chest heaving. "Claire?" he panted. "Where'd you go?" There hadn't been any shots fired. What could've happened?

She emerged from under one of the nearby desks with Khan in her arms. "Is it over?"

Emotion swelled in his chest. He nodded, opening his arms. "It's over. Thanks to that attack cat you're holding."

Weston laughed. "There I was, wondering if it was a good idea for you to bring him with us."

"Good boy. Good boy." Claire's tears soaked into

the cat's fur while Khan licked his paws like he hadn't done anything out of the ordinary, like he hadn't saved his owner's life.

Then again, Luke thought as he took them both in his arms, *it could've been pride in a job well done.* He thought it might've been, knowing the cat in question.

"I thought I was about to lose you." Now that it was over and he was holding her trembling body next to his, he could admit that much.

"You thought that? You thought it?" Her eyes were sharp when they met his, sharp enough to surprise him. "What did you think you were doing back there? Offering yourself up to him. You know he could've killed you, right?"

"I wouldn't have let that happen." He smoothed sweaty hair back from her forehead and cheeks. "So long as I knew he didn't have you in his crosshairs, I could've taken care of myself."

"You're sure about that?"

"You doubt me now, Kitten?" He pressed his lips to her forehead, eyes closed, thanking anything and anyone listening that the woman in his arms was exactly who she was.

Even now, having come so close to dying, she would think to scold him for putting himself in harm's way.

"Cops are a minute away," Brax announced with a satisfied smile.

That smile lasted only a second before the stairwell door burst open and a team of security guards poured onto the floor.

"So much for security." Chance smirked, his hands raised. He approached the men and explained what had taken place, that the police were on their way and all would be settled when they arrived.

Luke was only dimly aware of this as he held on to Claire. He had all he needed right there.

"Did you mean what you said?" Her voice was muffled, her mouth near his shoulder, but he heard the hope there.

"I said a lot of things. Which thing in particular?"

"You know what I'm talking about. Loving me." She lifted her head, her baby blues searching his. "Is that true?"

"You don't know by now?" He had to laugh in disbelief. "Do you think I go to these lengths for just anybody? Because I'll tell you right now, I don't. Only for people I love more than anything else in the world."

Tears filled her eyes, but they weren't the tears left behind after a close call.

They held joy. Wonder. He knew how she felt.

"You know I love you, too, right?" She giggled softly, a little giddy. "I can't believe I never said that before now. I just figured you knew."

He kissed her softly, tenderly, a kiss filled with every hope and dream he had for their life together.

And it would be spent together, because he couldn't remember how he'd lived without her.

And he certainly couldn't have imagined a future without her.

He didn't want to try.

But that would have to wait, since now the sound of sirens filled the air. They had some serious explaining to do to the police.

Chapter Twenty-Five

It was all so beautiful.

Claire had appreciated the beauty of the land surrounding the Pattersons' cabin during her first visit with Luke over six weeks ago. Even then, she'd been able to recognize how special a place it was. Peaceful and perfect, like the modern world hadn't quite made its way there yet.

Now? Without the threat of imminent death hanging over her head?

It might as well have been heaven.

Especially considering who was there with her.

"Fishing is actually a lot more fun than I ever imagined it would be." Claire cast off, waiting for the hook and fly to hit the water and send ripples out over the otherwise still lake. She reeled her line in just a little, knowing now that the motion would attract any nearby fish.

Luke had taught her a lot.

He smiled with a wry grin, careful to keep his voice soft to avoid scaring away the fish. "That's easy for you to say. You're a natural."

"I have a good teacher." And yes, she was slightly better at it than he was, which helped her enjoyment. But she wasn't about to say that out loud.

She loved him and knew he loved her and would forgive a lot of things, but there were times when a girl knew not to tread on a man's ego.

It had been a magical few days together for sure, and exactly what they both needed now that the hectic mess of clearing her name was over. Now it was nothing more than a memory.

Though it was still a fresh memory, she knew it would fade with time.

And Luke would help. Just the way he always did.

The information that she'd sent out to the police department had been more than enough to put Vance Ballard away for the rest of his life, along with the man who'd murdered Julia in such cold-blooded fashion.

There was plenty of additional evidence against Ballard's murderous bodyguard and the other one along with him. Julia's murder was only the tip of an iceberg that ran wide and deep. It was a comfort to know those men would get what they deserved. Even if it wouldn't bring back any of the lives they'd taken.

She drew a deep breath and let it out slowly, the way she always did whenever the still-fresh reality threatened to close in on her. How close she'd come to losing her life. Or, worse, to losing everything that had ever truly mattered.

Luke hadn't been lying that day, describing how she would suffer if he'd died because of her.

But he hadn't.

She took another deep breath and reminded herself it was safe to be happy. Safe to feel secure. Safe to feel loved.

The early-morning sun framed Luke's profile. He took her breath away, even after weeks of seeing him constantly. Would it always be like that?

"What are you thinking about?" He glanced her way with another little smile before reeling his line in just a bit to attract attention.

"Hmm? How did you know I was thinking about anything?"

"I know you, Kitten. That mind of yours never stops working." He smiled wider. "And I could feel you staring at me."

"Was I staring?"

"It sure felt that way."

She laughed at herself. "I guess you're nice to stare at."

"Thank you. You're not so bad yourself."

"Anyway," she continued, turning back to the water, "I was thinking about how grateful I am to have the cabin to ourselves for a little while. I know I've said it before, but your parents are the best."

"They know quality when they see it." He winked.

"Obviously, since they took to you the way they did."

"You're in a sweet-talking mood today. Not that I mind, of course."

"I guess I'm feeling generous since I've already

caught three fish, and you've caught… How many again?"

"Shush, woman. I should've known you would lord it over me."

She eventually stopped giggling. "Really. I meant what I said. You, your brothers… You're a special group. I never could've imagined them welcoming me the way they have." She didn't bother saying anything about what they'd done to ensure her safety. By then, they'd rehashed the details of that day at the Passage Digital office and the days leading up to it more than enough.

"They know quality when they see it, too."

"It's easy for you to brush it off—not that you're not taking me seriously or anything. I know you are. But you've known what it means to be part of a family a lot longer than I have. It's still new to me."

He kept his gaze trained on the water, speaking slowly. "You have all the time in the world to get used to it…if that's what you want."

If that was what she wanted? She wanted nothing more in the entire world than to be with Luke for the rest of her life. Longer than that, if possible. Forever.

But she wouldn't push for anything more than this. For now, this heavenly trip was more than enough. Focusing on just the two of them and being happy.

This time, she felt Luke's gaze on her instead of the other way around. "Where did you go?"

"You mean, other than right here? On the lake with you?"

He wasn't buying it. "Yes. Other than right here. You went someplace else."

Darn him for being so observant. "It'll take me some time to get used to living like a regular person, I think. I've spent so much of my life closed off from others. I didn't want to trust. I didn't want to run the risk of getting hurt. I figured it was easier on my own." She shrugged. "You know all this."

"I do. And I understand. It's not like I adjusted right away to knowing I had a family around me, either. It took time to get used to that new mindset." He offered a soft chuckle. "More than six weeks. In case you happen to find that relevant."

"Gee. Why would that matter?" They laughed together as softly as they could for the sake of the fish.

"So long as you're happy, Kitten. That's all I want."

And she knew it, and she loved him more than ever for it. Somebody in the world wanted her happiness above all else—her safety and well-being, her fulfillment.

The fact that this person happened to be Luke was the icing on the cake.

"I'm happy right now. I'm happy with you." She leaned over to kiss him, but the kiss was cut short by a tug on her line.

"Again?" Luke laughed, grabbing the net in case she needed help. She was much better at reeling her catch than she was at first, so there was no need for him to splash around in the water for her sake.

"What can I say?" She held up a sizable, shining, wriggling trout with a proud smile. There was no helping it.

"Are you putting something special on the hook? Are you bribing these fish?"

She laughed as he took the hook from the trout's mouth. That was something she still couldn't bring herself to do, even averting her eyes when he did it. Catching and cleaning and eating them was one thing.

There were limits, though.

"Yeah, I'm bribing them in some weird way so they'll bite. You figured out my trick."

"Are you sure you aren't, though?"

"What?" She looked his way when curiosity won out over squeamishness. "What are you talking about?"

"There's…something…else on the hook." Luke plopped the fish into the basket between them, then bent to rinse something off in the water.

"What is it? I didn't put anything special on there… You're right here with me, you see what I'm doing." Curious, she leaned over his shoulder.

He stood and turned to her.

And held out a ring.

She dropped her pole in favor of crossing her hands over her chest, where her heart had suddenly started pounding. "What…? How…? What…?"

Luke offered the sweetest smile. "Should I bother answering those questions?"

She couldn't answer. Somebody had stolen her words. All Claire could do was shake her head while her eyes remained glued to the ring. White gold. Diamond solitaire. Sparkling in the sunlight.

He lowered himself to one knee. "I didn't intend to do this here and now, but with the direction the conversation took, it seemed like a natural time to ask you to marry me."

She gulped. "Oh. My gosh."

"I'll take your reaction as surprise and not horror."

"Oh, no! Not horror. Definitely surprise." Her head felt like it was about to fall right off, she was so surprised.

"You didn't know I was planning to propose?"

"I hoped…" she admitted, trembling, "but I didn't know. I didn't want to assume anything."

"Which is one reason of many for me to ask you to marry me, Claire Wallace." There was so much love shining on his face, looking up at her the way he was, holding out the ring. "You've been the one for me all our lives. The one person I could never forget. You've always been part of my soul."

Her breath caught and her eyes filled with tears.

"You always will be," he murmured. "And I fully intend to spend the rest of my life reminding you of how lovable you are. Because you are. You're worthy of adoration and support and protection and everything I could ever offer. More than that, but I'm nothing special. I'm not a superhero, I swear. Though I'll do everything in my power to be that for you. I'll be anything and everything you need."

She shook her head as tears spilled over. "You're already everything I need and more than I ever dreamed I'd have. I don't think I could be happier than I am right now at this moment."

"Is that a yes?"

She giggled and nodded. "It's an absolute yes."

There was no time to say anything else before he was on his feet again and she was in his arms. He kissed her, filling her heart with so much love. And joy. And hope.

Finally, she had hope for her future.

And thanks to Luke, she had the courage to dream.

"I love you." He touched his forehead to hers while his arms locked tight around her, holding her close enough that she could feel his heart pound in time with hers. "Thank you for saying yes."

"I love you, too. Thank you for asking." She opened her eyes. "Wait. Where did the ring come from?"

"My pocket. Where do you think?" He laughed at himself. "I pulled it out when you were looking away. Come on, you have to give me points for originality."

"Oh, you definitely won some points."

"Speaking of which…" He took her left hand in his and slipped the cool band over her finger. It was a perfect fit.

Just like the two of them.

"There goes the rest of my day." Claire held out her hand, moving her finger, admiring the diamond's sparkle. "I don't think I'll be able to take my eyes off this ring."

"Wow. I killed two birds with one stone, then. No pun intended."

"What do you mean?"

He offered a wink, nodding to the poles lying on the ground. "If you're distracted, I might actually be able to catch more fish than you."

"Something tells me it'll take more than a sparkling diamond for you to manage that, Luke Patterson."

Still, she was willing to give him this one since he'd given her so much more. A lifetime's worth of more.

And they had only just begun.

* * * * *

USA TODAY *bestselling author Janie Crouch's*
miniseries San Antonio Security
continues next month with

Texas Bodyguard: Brax.

Look for it wherever Harlequin Intrigue
books are sold!

#2133 SET UP IN THE CITY
A Colt Brothers Investigation • by B.J. Daniels

All hell breaks loose when Willie Colt's extradited felon disappears. He knows he was set up, and he'll need big-city attorney Ellie Shaffer to prove it. But nothing—and no one—is what it seems. Soon the dangerous truth about their connection to the criminal is revealed...

#2134 RESCUED BY THE RANCHER
The Cowboys of Cider Creek • by Barb Han

When rancher Callum Hayes opens his home to Payton Reinert, he knows she's the only woman who escaped the Masked Monster alive. But how far will Callum go to protect her from a deranged killer determined that she won't escape a second time?

#2135 SHOT IN THE DARK
Covert Cowboy Soldiers • by Nicole Helm

Hardened ex-marine Henry Thompson is no babysitter. But when Jessie Peterson begs for his help locating her rebellious daughter, his military-rescue instincts kick in. Family treasure, secret doppelgängers and dogged gunfire are no match for Henry's guard. Jessie, however, is another story...

#2136 TEXAS BODYGUARD: BRAX
San Antonio Security • by Janie Crouch

When security specialist Brax Patterson gains custody of his nephew, nanny Tessa Mahoney is a godsend. But his beautiful, secretive employee is more than she seems...and brings danger to Brax's front door. Is Tessa an innocent victim of the cartel he's investigating or the one pulling all the strings?

#2137 CATCHING THE CARLING LAKE KILLER
West Investigations • by K.D. Richards

Journalist Simone Jarrett is haunted by the murder she witnessed years ago. But instead of closure, her return to Carling Lake brings her Sheriff Lance Webb. With the body count climbing, Lance fears the Card Killer is back to terrorize the woman who got away.

#2138 RESOLUTE AIM
The Protectors of Boone County, Texas • by Leslie Marshman

Deputy Noah Reed has always been a risk-taker—the exact opposite of his trigger-shy new partner. But Bree Delgado is no green cop. With a meth ring exposed and drug runners out for revenge, the bad boy out to make good will have to trust her to protect his back...and his heart.

YOU CAN FIND MORE INFORMATION ON UPCOMING HARLEQUIN TITLES, FREE EXCERPTS AND MORE AT HARLEQUIN.COM.

HICNM0223

Get 4 FREE REWARDS!

We'll send you 2 FREE Books plus 2 FREE Mystery Gifts.

EAGLE MOUNTAIN CLIFFHANGER — CINDI MYERS

PRESUMED DEAD — NICHOLE SEVERN

FREE Value Over **$20**

KILLER IN THE HEARTLAND — CARLA CASSIDY

CAVANAUGH JUSTICE: UP CLOSE AND DEADLY — MARIE FERRARELLA

Both the **Harlequin Intrigue®** and **Harlequin® Romantic Suspense** series feature compelling novels filled with heart-racing action-packed romance that will keep you on the edge of your seat.

YES! Please send me 2 FREE novels from the Harlequin Intrigue or Harlequin Romantic Suspense series and my 2 FREE gifts (gifts are worth about $10 retail). After receiving them, if I don't wish to receive any more books, I can return the shipping statement marked "cancel." If I don't cancel, I will receive 6 brand-new Harlequin Intrigue Larger-Print books every month and be billed just $6.49 each in the U.S. or $6.99 each in Canada, a savings of at least 13% off the cover price, or 4 brand-new Harlequin Romantic Suspense books every month and be billed just $5.49 each in the U.S. or $6.24 each in Canada, a savings of at least 12% off the cover price. It's quite a bargain! Shipping and handling is just 50¢ per book in the U.S. and $1.25 per book in Canada.* I understand that accepting the 2 free books and gifts places me under no obligation to buy anything. I can always return a shipment and cancel at any time by calling the number below. The free books and gifts are mine to keep no matter what I decide.

Choose one: ☐ **Harlequin Intrigue**
Larger-Print
(199/399 HDN GRJK)

☐ **Harlequin Romantic Suspense**
(240/340 HDN GRJK)

Name (please print)

Address — Apt. #

City — State/Province — Zip/Postal Code

Email: Please check this box ☐ if you would like to receive newsletters and promotional emails from Harlequin Enterprises ULC and its affiliates. You can unsubscribe anytime.

Mail to the Harlequin Reader Service:
IN U.S.A.: P.O. Box 1341, Buffalo, NY 14240-8531
IN CANADA: P.O. Box 603, Fort Erie, Ontario L2A 5X3

Want to try 2 free books from another series! Call 1-800-873-8635 or visit www.ReaderService.com.

*Terms and prices subject to change without notice. Prices do not include sales taxes, which will be charged (if applicable) based on your state or country of residence. Canadian residents will be charged applicable taxes. Offer not valid in Quebec. This offer is limited to one order per household. Books received may not be as shown. Not valid for current subscribers to the Harlequin Intrigue or Harlequin Romantic Suspense series. All orders subject to approval. Credit or debit balances in a customer's account(s) may be offset by any other outstanding balance owed by or to the customer. Please allow 4 to 6 weeks for delivery. Offer available while quantities last.

Your Privacy—Your information is being collected by Harlequin Enterprises ULC, operating as Harlequin Reader Service. For a complete summary of the information we collect, how we use this information and to whom it is disclosed, please visit our privacy notice located at corporate.harlequin.com/privacy-notice. From time to time we may also exchange your personal information with reputable third parties. If you wish to opt out of this sharing of your personal information, please visit readerservice.com/consumerschoice or call 1-800-873-8635. **Notice to California Residents**—Under California law, you have specific rights to control and access your data. For more information on these rights and how to exercise them, visit corporate.harlequin.com/california-privacy.

HIHRS22R3

HARLEQUIN
PLUS

Try the best multimedia subscription service for romance readers like you!

Read, Watch and Play.

Experience the easiest way to get the romance content you crave.

Start your **FREE TRIAL** at
<u>www.harlequinplus.com/freetrial</u>.